A JAILBIRD IN THE VISION IS WORTH TWO IN THE PRISON

PIPER ASHWELL PSYCHIC P.I., BOOK 6

KELLY HASHWAY

Cover design ©Red Umbrella Graphic Designs

To Ayla with love

CHAPTER ONE

The bakery counter at Marcia's Nook is crowded for a Tuesday morning, so I head to the mystery section of the bookstore and wait for the line to clear. It might seem odd to some people that I choose to spend my free time reading about murders when most days I'm working murder cases alongside the Weltunkin PD, but what can I say? I'm not exactly your typical private investigator. Being psychic and having a special talent for psychometry, the ability to read the energy off objects, means being in physical contact with people is difficult for me. Books, on the other hand, are my source of comfort—along with toasted almond coffee and my sweet golden retriever, Jezebel.

"Haven't you read all the books in this section by now?"

I turn around at the sound of my partner's voice. Mitchell Brennan is a detective with the Weltunkin PD.

He also happens to be my best friend, even though he pushes my buttons more than anyone else I know. "You do understand how bookstores work, right? They get new shipments of books in all the time."

"If you actually watched TV like a normal human being, you wouldn't spend so much of your paycheck in this place." He reaches around me and plucks a book off the shelf. "Here. You haven't read this one yet."

It's a little disturbing how well he knows me, but he spends more time *with* me than without considering we work together and he spends most nights at my apartment so we can discuss cases. We're both married to our jobs. The truly disturbing thing is that my dog is in love with Mitchell, even though I'm the one who rescued her after her former owner was murdered.

I flip the book over and scan the blurb on the back cover. Satisfied I'll enjoy the story, I head back toward the bakery counter.

"I already placed our order and paid. Marcia should have it ready for us," Mitchell says.

"Great. I'm starving."

Mitchell smirks. "I told you you'd be starving this morning after only eating wonton soup for dinner."

"It's not my fault someone forgot the egg rolls."

He holds up his hands in front of him. "I offered to go back and get them. You were the one who said no."

We stop in front of the bakery counter, where Marcia

is shaking her head at us. "What did you do this time, Detective?" she asks.

"He let me starve," I say.

"You said—"

I hold up my hand to silence Mitchell. "Marcia, if you showed up at my apartment with wonton soup and forgot the egg rolls, what would you do?"

"Go back to get the egg rolls."

"I offered. She said no," Mitchell protests.

Marcia cocks her head. "Really, Detective, I'm disappointed you couldn't figure this one out. She said no, but the right thing for you to do would have been to go anyway."

"How do you figure? She said no." He looks back and forth between us.

"It's not a wonder this one is single." I hitch my thumb in Mitchell's direction, and Marcia laughs.

"You two make my mornings. Seriously." She pushes the bag of pastries and the drink caddy across the counter toward us. "You are going to carry these for Piper, aren't you, Detective?" she prods.

"Women," Mitchell mutters as he grabs the food and drinks.

"I hope your day gets better, Detective," Marcia says as he heads for the door.

I place my book on the counter. "He's so easy to mess with," I say, whipping out my phone to pay.

She rings me up and looks over my shoulder. "I'd cut

him some slack for the rest of the day. The poor man looks rattled."

I peer over my shoulder to see Mitchell is awkwardly holding his phone in the same hand as the bag of pastries. Must be someone from the station messaging him about a new case.

I turn back to Marcia. "He's in luck since it looks like we just got a new case." I grab the book and give her a small wave.

"Good luck," she calls after me.

Mitchell's brow is furrowed as I approach, so I ask, "Something wrong?"

"Maybe. Wallace texted me that you and I need to get to the station as soon as possible."

"No reason why?"

He shakes his head as he uses his back to open the door. He holds it for me to exit first.

"That's odd. Doesn't Wallace usually call you instead of texting?"

"Yeah, that's what's throwing me off."

I nod. "Because it means he doesn't want to tell you what it's about over the phone."

The twenty-three steps to my office pass quickly, and I open the door, which is unlocked, indicating my dad is already here for the day.

"Good morning, pumpkin," he says as I step inside.

"Morning, Dad." I place my purse on my desk.

Mitchell puts the drink caddy and bag down on Dad's

oversized desk. "I'm calling him," he says, already bringing the phone to his ear.

"Who?" Dad asks, looking at me.

"Officer Wallace texted asking Mitchell and me to come to the station as soon as possible. He didn't say why."

Dad nods. "That means the chief probably told him to get you both there."

Why wouldn't Chief Johansen call Mitchell himself?

"Wallace, it's Brennan. What's going on?" Mitchell's eyes narrow. "All right. Tell him we're on our way." He hangs up and turns to Dad. "You're right. Chief Johansen wants Piper and me, and he's not telling anyone at the station why."

"Well, that can't be good," I say.

"Want me to tag along?" Dad asks. Everyone at the station, including the chief, loves Dad. He was the best detective at the Weltunkin PD right up to the day he retired.

"No, I think Piper and I should go on our own. We'll let you know what it's about as soon as we can, though."

Dad reaches inside the pastry bag and removes a chocolate glazed donut. Then he removes one of the coffees from the drink caddy. "All yours," he says.

Mitchell grabs the rest, and we head out for the station.

I make it a point to avoid the Weltunkin police station unless it's absolutely necessary to go there. While most of the officers are pretty indifferent to me, there's one who tries to make my life as miserable as possible. Officer Andrews has no problem using me when it benefits him, like when I found out his wife isn't planning to leave him despite his history of cheating and visiting strip clubs, but he also hates me for having read him against his will and being privy to his dark secrets. I'm just hoping I won't have to see him while we're there.

Officer Wallace is the first to greet us when we arrive. Him I like, and it's not just because his partner is the very adorable and smart K9, Harry. Officer Wallace is actually impressed by my abilities.

"Hey, Piper. Hey, Mitchell," Officer Wallace says. "Sorry I couldn't tell you more on the phone, but I honestly don't know anything. The chief just told me to get you both down here."

"No problem," Mitchell says. "I take it the chief is in his office."

Officer Wallace nods, and we head for the office in the back of the station, but I can't help noticing Officer Gilbert, a newbie on the force, is sitting with Officer Andrews.

"Is he still in training?" I whisper to Mitchell, not wanting Officer Andrews to hear me.

"Yeah, and he was officially named Andrews's partner a few days ago."

"I guess he drew the unlucky short stick," I say.

He nods. "But it's kind of funny considering Gilbert idolizes your father. He spends most of his time bringing up cases your dad worked on, which means Andrews spends most of his time rolling his eyes."

I smile. "Well, that's got to be entertaining."

Mitchell stops in front of the chief's door. The walls to his office are glass, but he has the blinds down. Mitchell raises his hand and knocks.

"Come in," Chief Johansen says in his deep voice.

Mitchell opens the door, and the fact that he steps into the office first makes me question if he thinks he'll need to protect me from what the chief is about to say.

"Have a seat," Chief Johansen says, his face void of emotion. Maybe it's my nerves, but somehow, he seems even taller than usual today. More so once I sit down. "There's no easy way to say this, so I'm just going to dive right in. I got a phone call today from a lawyer whose client is interested in enlisting your help, Ms. Ashwell."

My help? Then why did the chief call Mitchell in here as well. "I'm sorry, but something isn't adding up. First, why me? Second, why wouldn't this client call me himself instead of going through his lawyer and you? And third, why is Mitchell here if this concerns my services and not the Weltunkin PD's?"

Chief Johansen leans forward in his chair. "I see you're not the type to sit back and wait for an explanation. You want to get right to the questions on your mind."

I take it that's his way of telling me not to interrupt him, so I don't respond.

"First, this isn't a typical situation in that the client isn't able to reach out to you on his own."

"Why is that?" I blurt out before I can realize I'm interrupting him again.

The chief's nostrils actually flare. "The man is currently residing in the Weltunkin prison after being convicted of murder."

A laugh escapes my lips. "I'm sorry, but he's in prison?"

"That's correct. And Detective Brennan is present because given the fact that one of our officers put this man behind bars, we want one of our own to handle this case with you every step along the way."

"This prisoner, I'm assuming he knows what I can do," I say.

The chief nods.

Mitchell whips out his pad and pen. "What's his name?"

"Levi O'Neil," Chief Johansen says, and the look on Mitchell's face would have clued me in to a few things even if my senses didn't step in at that particular moment.

"Officer Andrews is the one who put him in jail," I say, knowing it's true.

"And that is why he will be nowhere near this investigation."

Chief Johansen couldn't have said anything else to make me happier.

"That won't be an issue," I say. "So, what does Mr. O'Neil want my help with exactly?"

"Finding and locking up his accomplice."

Mitchell sits up straight. "No way. You'd be putting Piper in the middle of a war between two criminals."

"I'm well aware." The expression on Chief Johansen's face is making it clear he doesn't have a problem with putting my life on the line.

CHAPTER TWO

So many things about this are bothering me right now. If I take this case, I'll have to reopen yet another of Officer Andrews's cases, which will only make him hate me more. Of course, I haven't yet decided if that's a positive or negative.

"Piper, you can turn this down," Mitchell says. "You're under no obligation to take the case. The man is behind bars. He's been sitting in prison for five years. There's no way he wouldn't say something until now if it were true."

"You don't believe that," I say. He's trying to protect me, but I'm not going to say that out loud in front of the chief. I look at Chief Johansen. "Let me see the case file. I'll go over it and decide if I want to hear what Mr. O'Neil has to say."

"Fair enough." Chief Johansen nods once in my

direction, and I get the sense he expected as much from me.

"Piper, can I speak with you in private for a moment?" Mitchell asks, getting to his feet.

Chief Johansen cocks his head at Mitchell, his expression saying so much with no words at all.

"I mean, if we're dismissed," Mitchell says.

"You are. Brennan, you can get the case file for Ms. Ashwell once you've had your little talk, and I'll expect to be kept up-to-date on this investigation."

I stand up, noticing Chief Johansen seems pretty insistent that I take the case. Why would he want me to help a convicted felon of all people? It doesn't make sense, which means I must be missing something.

Mitchell brings me to his desk and speaks in hushed tones, probably because we have the attention of all the officers in the station, seeing as we just had a private meeting with the chief. "You do not want to get involved in this. The case is closed. The right guy is behind bars. There is absolutely no reason to go to that prison and speak with O'Neil."

"What does O'Neil want with you?" Officer Andrews asks from behind me.

Mitchell raises his head and glares at him. "This doesn't concern you, Andrews."

"If we're talking about Levi O'Neil, then it does. I put him behind bars. It was my case, not yours, Brennan."

Andrews hates that Mitchell is lead detective on all the really big cases.

"He's going to hear about this eventually," I tell Mitchell before turning to face Officer Andrews. "O'Neil asked to speak with me because he's claiming he didn't work alone and there's a killer on the loose."

Officer Andrews laughs. "And you fell for that? The guy got busted and is facing a life sentence. You can't possibly believe he's telling the truth." Officer Andrews crosses his arms and cocks his head at me. "Your so-called psychic abilities should be cluing you in on the fact that this guy is messing with you because he, like many others, thinks you're a fraud."

I stand up and face him. Now a nice person would probably not consider airing Officer Andrews's dirty laundry in front of a police station full of cops, but one of my issues as a psychic is people's emotions tend to rub off on me. Since my grandmother was an empath, that's not uncommon. And right now, I'm channeling Officer Andrews's dickheadedness. "My *so-called psychic abilities* are the reason you're still married even though you're a lowlife, cheating bastard who can't stay away from strip clubs."

A few nearby officers gasp. Not that I don't believe they didn't already suspect as much, but like I said, the average person wouldn't have called out Officer Andrews on this in his place of work.

"You're a fake, Ashwell. Nothing but a fraud who spews lies about people. If you ask me—"

"No one did," Mitchell interrupts, also on his feet now.

I raise my hand to Mitchell. I can fight my own battles. "Go on," I tell Officer Andrews, because I'm interested to see how far he'll go with this.

"If you ask me, you're nothing more than a perceptive person who pieces a few clues together and pretends the information came to you in visions. Like that guy from the TV show *Psych*."

"Great show," Officer Gilbert says, coming up alongside Officer Andrews, a WPD coffee mug in hand. "I binge watched all eight seasons." He's smiling like he has no clue there's a verbal war going on three feet in front of him.

A huge part of me is dying to latch onto Officer Andrews's arm and read him against his will, but with his current mood, I don't doubt he'll cuff me for assault. I settle for saying, "Tell your better half—and I'm referring to your wife, not the redhead named Candy at the strip club—I'll be solving yet another case you couldn't handle on your own." I turn and walk out of the police station. Why I still go there is beyond me.

I walk to Mitchell's patrol car and wait by the passenger door. He doesn't emerge for a few minutes, which means he has a few choice words for Officer

Andrews as well. Mitchell unlocks the patrol car the second he steps out of the station, and I get inside without saying anything.

Mitchell starts the car and says, "Weltunkin prison?"

I nod. I need to hear what O'Neil has to say. If there really is a killer out there and I don't do something about it, any murder victim that turns up could be on my hands. I'm not about to let that happen. I finish my coffee, which is now cold in the cup holder. I'm in it for the caffeine boost, so I down the contents anyway and eat my donut. I don't want to be hangry while questioning a convicted felon.

Mitchell's badge and my P.I. license get us through the security clearance at the prison, and we head into the area where visitors can speak to inmates. Mitchell and I sit down in front of the glass separating us from Levi O'Neil. He's a big guy with a bald head and quite possibly the prettiest blue eyes I've ever seen. They sort of draw you in, and I can't help wondering if he used them to his advantage to lure his victim right to him.

O'Neil picks up the phone on his side of the glass, and being that Mitchell knows I'm not about to touch the one on our side and spark a vision of who knows what, he picks it up and holds it between us so we both can hear.

"I didn't think you'd actually show," O'Neil says in a voice that's much higher pitched than I anticipated.

"Why did you request to speak to me?" I ask.

"So, it was curiosity that brought you in. I figured you'd had a psychic vision and already knew why I wanted to talk to you."

He's a believer but falsely thinks I can see whatever I want to. Sometimes that's worse than working with a total skeptic. "Mr. O'Neil—"

He laughs, cutting me off. "I don't think anyone's called me Mr. since I was put in here. The orange jumpsuit seems to strip you of receiving any form of respect, so thank you for actually showing some."

I'd think it was his crime that stripped him of any form of respect, but I don't say that. "Mr. O'Neil, my abilities don't just show me things at will. It's a little more complicated than that. Why don't you tell me why you requested this meeting, and we'll go from there?"

"Fair enough." He adjusts his grip on the phone and cracks his neck before beginning. "Are you familiar with my case?"

"Not at all," I admit. "I wanted to talk to you before reading the case file."

He laughs. "Was that so you weren't swayed by what you read? I'm sure you usually side with the WPD."

"Actually, if I'm being honest, I don't care much at all for the arresting officer on your case."

He smiles. "Well, then we have that in common."

"I suppose we do. Why don't you rehash the case for me in your own words?"

"No can do. I'm not going to tell you what really happened."

"Then why are we here?" Mitchell asks.

O'Neil leans toward the glass and studies Mitchell's face. "I don't even know who you are."

"Detective Mitchell Brennan. I'm Piper's partner."

O'Neil looks at me. "Seriously? Why this guy?"

This time I'm the one who laughs. "I ask myself that question every day."

"I like you, Ashwell," O'Neil says.

O'Neil can definitely be charming when he wants to be, but I'm getting the sense he knows that and he used it to his advantage when it came to kidnapping the woman he or his accomplice murdered. "You know we don't exactly have all the time in the world here." I look around at the guards observing the interactions. "Let's cut to the chase."

"Look into the case. I know you'll figure it out. I can't tell you anything, but the fact that I went to prison alone should clue you in on that much. I will give you a hint, though." He holds up two fingers. "Two birds with one stone."

Oh, goodie. We're going to talk in riddles. I roll my eyes. Two criminals. I've got that much. "Tell me something I don't know."

"Dead women can still talk, but a dead bird can't sing." He smiles, hangs up the phone, and walks back to the guard.

Mitchell hangs up the phone. "What the hell was that supposed to mean?"

I take a deep breath, contemplating O'Neil's words. "Was his victim's body found?"

"No. He confessed to the murder but said we'd never find her."

"Then he wants me to find her body and read it. That's what he meant by 'Dead women can still talk.'" She can talk to me in the form of a vision.

"What about the dead bird part?" Mitchell asks.

I shrug because I have no idea what he meant by that. "I need to read the case file. We'll start there."

"You're really going to reopen this case?"

I stand up. "I don't see any other option. If there's a second guilty party—one O'Neil is clearly afraid of even from the safety of his cell—then I need to find him."

"You think he confessed to the murder because he was afraid of what would happen to him if he didn't take the fall?" Mitchell asks, walking with me back to his car.

"It's the only thing that makes sense to me."

He shoves his hands into his pockets as we walk. "O'Neil is huge, a force to be reckoned with. I'd hate to see what the guy he's afraid of looks like."

We reach the car, but before I get in I say, "Well, buckle up, Detective, because if I have anything to say about it, we're going to find out."

Mitchell drops me off at my office and opts to grab the case file from the station on his own. It's not that I'm afraid to face Officer Andrews. Not at all. In fact, I welcome the opportunity to watch him squirm. But Mitchell thinks if I go to the station and retrieve the file for yet another one of Officer Andrews's cases, he'll wind up making the entire station miserable for the rest of the day. He's like a giant toddler who throws temper tantrums whenever he doesn't get his way.

Dad and I head to the sub shop to pick up lunch for the three of us before jumping into the few details of the case we actually have. I know he's itching to find out what Mitchell and I learned down at the prison, but he waits until we're back in the office to start questioning me.

"What's O'Neil like?" Dad asks me, handing me my unsweetened iced tea and an Italian hero.

"Kind of odd. He wants my help, but he's not willing to give me anything to go on. He was practically talking in riddles."

"You think he's afraid of what will happen if he gives you anything concrete to go on?" Dad takes a bite of his pickle and washes it down with lemonade.

I nod. "The only clue he gave me was, 'Dead women can still talk, but a dead bird can't sing.'"

Dad's brow furrows. "Well, the dead woman part I get considering you can read the body."

I shudder. "Not really what I want to do, though."

He reaches over and places his hand on mine. He knows to only touch my left hand so as not to spark a vision.

"What's with the bird reference?" I ask. I've never tried to read a bird before, but I imagine the visions would be the same whether the bird was alive or dead.

Mitchell opens the door and walks in with a case file in his hand. "Wow. You would not believe what a giant spectacle that was."

"It didn't go any better without me there?" I ask.

Mitchell sits down in the seat across from me and tosses the file onto the desk. "Not really. Andrews tried to tell the chief he should be the one on this case, and when the chief said you were our best option, Andrews completely lost it. I felt bad for Gilbert because as Andrews's new partner, he felt the need to support him, but you could tell he has more faith in you solving this case." Mitchell reaches for his sandwich and immediately digs in.

It's nice to know Officer Gilbert will be a friendly face at the station, but I can see how that will cause more trouble between Officer Andrews and me.

"What were you two discussing before I got here?"

"I was just filling Dad in on our conversation with O'Neil. If you can call it that since he barely said anything."

"The riddle is definitely interesting," Dad says,

rewrapping the second half of his sandwich. Mom must have put him on a diet now that he's not actively running around chasing criminals. Poor Dad. He's not overweight by any means.

"I had a thought," Mitchell says before sipping his lemonade. "What if the bird he mentioned is him?"

"Like a jailbird," I say.

Mitchell points to me and nods.

"He can't sing if he's dead. Meaning if he talks, his former partner will kill him." I widen my eyes at Mitchell. "That was really insightful."

He smiles. "Thank you."

"Then that would mean he's dead set on me finding the body and reading it."

"Sorry, pumpkin," Dad says.

"Tell me what we know about the victim." I try to eat my sandwich, but my stomach is already churning at the prospect of reading another dead body.

Mitchell leans forward and opens the case file. "Amelia Crane was a twenty-three-year-old actress. She performed in several plays at the playhouse right here in town. She was a singer, too. She lived alone in an apartment above the dry cleaner."

"Do you have a photograph?" I ask. It helps to be able to picture a person if I'm going to get a good read on them.

"Here." Mitchell removes a small photograph from the file and hands it to me.

Amelia had blonde hair and green eyes, but it's hard to

focus on her image in the picture because my eyes immediately go to the bird cage behind her. The bird isn't visible, which means Amelia's body is blocking it. I let out a sigh. "Well, Mitchell, as insightful as your observation of O'Neil being the bird in the riddle was, you were wrong."

"What do you mean?" He cocks his head at me.

I toss the picture onto my desk and tap the bird cage. "Amelia Crane had a pet bird."

"Why would O'Neil mention Amelia's pet?" Mitchell picks up the photograph and brings it closer to his face.

"Do you think the bird is somehow important to the case?" Dad asks me.

My senses never mislead me. They might confuse the hell out of me at times, but the way they zeroed in on the bird cage means it's important. And right now, it's the only lead I have. "Dad, I need you to find out what happened to Amelia's bird after O'Neil confessed to killing her."

Mitchell puts the photograph down and meets my gaze. "You're going to read the bird, aren't you?"

"If it's still alive, yes. Like O'Neil said, dead birds can't sing." Though I'm still not sure about that.

"Unless we're dealing with a *Pet Sematary* situation here."

Dad and I both roll our eyes.

"What?" Mitchell shrugs. "Of course, we can't even see the bird in this picture. It's possible she didn't have one. Maybe she just had the bird cage for décor."

"What do you know about décor?" I ask.

"I watch HGTV with Jez sometimes. If you weren't always reading, you'd probably notice."

"Okay, back to the case," Dad says, refereeing as usual. "I can't believe I'm saying this, but we have a bird to track down."

CHAPTER THREE

Amelia Crane doesn't appear to have many living relatives in Weltunkin. She grew up here, but her parents both died in a car accident when she was seventeen. She lived with her aunt and uncle for a year before getting her own apartment. I'm assuming her aunt and uncle would have gotten Amelia's belongings after O'Neil confessed to killing her, so I look up their phone numbers.

"We'll start here," I say, shutting my laptop and handing the slip of paper with the two numbers to Dad. "Will you call them and set up a meeting?" Dad's best with people, so I figure he should be the one to make contact with them.

"I have an address," Mitchell says. "I'm putting it into my navigation right now. It's on a back road I'm not that familiar with."

"I need to head home to walk Jez before we go talk to the Cranes." I grab my purse.

"I'll drive you," Mitchell says.

Dad picks up his phone. "I'll try to set up a meeting right away. I'll call you as soon as I get off the phone with them."

We leave Dad, and Mitchell drives to my apartment. He keeps giving me sideways glances, but he never actually says anything for the entire ride. It's more than a little annoying, but I don't bother asking what's on his mind. He'll come out with it when he's ready.

Jez greets us with big tail wags. After saying hello to her, I immediately fill her water bowl, knowing Mitchell will take her for a walk. I think he enjoys walking her as much as she enjoys it.

I look out the window to see them on the sidewalk, Mitchell bending down to scratch behind Jez's ears. She licks him straight up the center of his face, making him laugh.

My phone rings, and I hurry to the kitchen to retrieve it from my purse. "Hey, Dad," I answer after reading his name on my screen. "What do you have for me?"

"Rebecca works from home and said we're welcome to come by at any time, but Jacob Crane gets off work at six, so if we want to talk to them both, we'll have to wait until then."

I check the clock on the stove. It's nearly five o'clock. How do the days get away from me like this? "Okay, let's plan to meet there around 5:30. That way I'll have time to read something of Amelia's before we talk to Jacob and Rebecca."

"I'll call Rebecca back and let her know," Dad says.

"Thanks. Do you want me to call Mom and tell her we'll be late for dinner?"

"Would you mind? She always goes easier on you than me." He chuckles.

"Sure thing. I'll call her now. Bye, Dad."

"Bye, pumpkin."

I dial Mom.

"Don't even tell me you're going to be late," she answers. "I have a turkey in the oven."

"I'm sorry, Mom. We have to question two people. We'll be there as soon as we can."

"And how soon do you actually think that will be, so I have an idea?" she asks.

"Sometime around six thirty. Definitely before seven."

"Don't blame me if you wind up eating cold turkey sandwiches instead of the meal I planned."

"I'm sure it will be delicious however we eat it. Love you," I add before ending the call.

Mitchell and Jez return, and with one look at my face, he says, "Let me guess. We're going to be late for dinner, and your mom isn't happy in the least."

"You got it. Dad set up a meeting for 5:30. Rebecca Crane is home now, but her husband will be home from work around six."

"I'm assuming the plan is to hopefully find the bird cage or something else of Amelia's for you to read and then question the Cranes afterward to fill in any gaps from your vision."

I bend down to kiss Jezebel on top of her head. "I think Mitchell is stepping up his game seeing as how smart you are. You're a good influence on him."

"I would complain, but Jez is extremely smart," Mitchell says. "You ready? We should probably get on the road."

"Yeah, let's go." I grab my purse. "Bye, Jez." I pause. "On second thought, let's drop her off with my mom on the way."

"We actually will be going by your parents' house, so it makes sense." Mitchell grabs Jez's leash and hooks her up.

It's good for people in my apartment building to see Jez in Mitchell's patrol car considering my landlord, Theodore Hall, told them she's a police dog. It was the only way to get around the "no pets" rule, and seeing as Mr. Hall is good friends with my father, it seemed like the best solution at the time.

Mom is happy to see Jez, as always. Even Max, my parents' dog, comes running to greet her. Max never cared for me before I got Jez, mostly because I could always tell when he was about to get into trouble. But he's been much better behaved now that he hangs out with Jez, and that's made him warm up to me as well.

I bend down and pat his head. "Hey, Max. How are

you doing, little man?" I hold out my hand, and he slaps his paw onto my palm. "Good boy!"

"Can you believe, after all these years, he's finally obeying commands?" Mom asks. "His playdates with Jezebel are really improving his overall demeanor."

"I'm happy to hear it. Jez loves them, too."

"It smells incredible, Mrs. Ashwell. I almost want to tell Piper to take the patrol car and go on without me."

Mom smiles at Mitchell. "I've turned the oven temperature down to attempt to slow the cooking process, but I'd do your best to make this a speedy interrogation."

"No one's interrogating anyone, Mom. We're going to speak with the victim's family." I stand back up and remove Jez's leash, which I hand to Mom.

Mom shoos us out the door. "Well, get a move on. I'm putting the food on the table at 6:45 with or without you. Max, Jezebel, and I will eat on our own if need be."

"We'll be here," Mitchell says, rubbing his stomach.

I have to practically push him to the car to make him leave.

"I swear everything your mom makes is incredible," he says once we're on the road.

"No argument from me."

"Why did the cooking gene skip you?" he asks, a subtle smirk on his lips.

"Who said it did?"

"Come on. When do you ever cook?"

"I live alone. Cooking for one doesn't really make sense. I'd be eating the same food for days on end."

"Not if you invite me over."

"When are you not over?"

"See, you'd be cooking for the both of us."

I shake my head at him. "Just drive, Detective."

Jacob and Rebecca Crane live in a huge house perched on a small hill. The driveway must be half a mile long. We pass a pond with one of those bridges so you can walk across it. There's also a big fenced-in area that makes me think they might have a horse or two. The house itself is a big farmhouse.

"Why would Amelia move out of a great place like this to live in a tiny apartment?" Mitchell asks as he parks in the circular driveway.

"No idea, but we don't exactly know what kind of people her aunt and uncle are yet."

He opens his door and meets me around the front of the car. "Are you sensing Amelia didn't get along with them?"

I'm not getting a sense of Amelia at all yet. "I'm just speculating."

He gives me a brief nod before walking up to the front door and ringing the bell.

Dad pulls up and parks behind Mitchell as the front door opens. I give him a wave before turning to face the woman in the doorway. Rebecca Crane is a small woman in her thirties. Her long blonde hair reaches to her waist.

My first instinct is that Jacob Crane must also be young. But if that's the case, I'd think Amelia would like living with her aunt and uncle. Of course, the other possibility is that Jacob married a woman much younger than he is and Amelia hated that.

I reach my hand out to shake Rebecca's, wanting to clear up that mystery right away so I know what I'm walking into. "Mrs. Crane, I'm Piper Ashwell."

"Why would the police be looking into Amelia's case after five years? O'Neil is locked up," Rebecca says into the phone.

"I don't know, sweetheart. I just hope they don't plan to make us rehash all of this. It was difficult enough the first time around."

Rebecca tugs her hand from mine and cocks her head at me.

"Sorry, I sort of zoned out for a moment," I say.

"Zoned out?" Rebecca looks to Mitchell. "Does she do that often?"

"I'm Detective Mitchell Brennan with the Weltunkin PD."

"And I'm Thomas Ashwell," Dad says, stepping right up and extending his hand. "We spoke on the phone."

"Yes." Her brow furrows. "Ashwell." She looks back and forth between Dad and me. "You're a father and daughter team?"

"We are," I say.

"May we please come in?" Dad asks.

She steps aside. "Of course." She's still looking at me like I'm crazy. Maybe the comment about zoning out wasn't the best way to cover up what I was really doing. Although, I'm starting to think she'd be even less inclined to handle the truth.

The house is immaculate, and since I know Rebecca works from home, I'm going to assume she has a housekeeper. What I find odd is that there are tons of photographs, but none include Amelia. Not that she lived here for long, but still.

"Before we ask you any questions, I was wondering if we could see the room where Amelia stayed when she was living here."

Rebecca's mouth hangs open. "Oh. Um, that was years ago. The room is now my husband's study."

"I see. Do you happen to have anything of Amelia's? I'm assuming her belongings were sent here after..." I don't want to upset her by mentioning the murder, but the more I study her features, the more I think she wasn't all that distraught over Amelia's passing.

"No. We donated all of Amelia's things to charity."

"What about her bird?" Mitchell asks.

Rebecca furrows her brow and shakes her head. "She didn't have a bird that I knew of."

I'm really hoping Jacob will be more helpful once he gets home, because it seems like Rebecca didn't know Amelia well at all.

"How long did she live here?" Mitchell asks.

"Less than a year. It was her senior year of high school, so she wasn't around much. You know how teenagers are." She waves a hand through the air, dismissing the thought.

"I'd still like to see her former room if that's okay," I say. There might be something left over that will give me a read on Amelia.

"Follow me." I expect Rebecca to lead us upstairs, but instead, she brings us to a room in the back of the house. She opens the door. "The room has its own entrance. That's why Amelia wanted it. We didn't protest because it meant that she didn't wake us up when she came home late."

"She didn't have a curfew?" Dad asks.

"Heavens no. She wasn't exactly our daughter. We didn't feel it was right to impose rules like that on her. She was practically an adult."

And barely younger than Rebecca.

"May I?" I ask, gesturing to the inside of the room.

"By all means." Rebecca crosses her arms as if she feels my need to look around is completely pointless.

It might be. All that's in here is a large bookshelf with accounting books on it, a desk, and a black leather couch. Nothing in here looks like it ever belonged to a seventeen-year-old girl.

"Do you happen to know which organization came to take the belongings from Amelia's apartment?" I ask.

"My husband took care of all the arrangements," she says without an ounce of emotion.

Did she not care about her niece at all?

"You said he'd be home by six?" Dad asks, checking his watch.

"Usually, yes. I could give him a call and find out for sure if you'd like." Mrs. Crane reaches for her phone in the front pocket of her black dress pants, and for the first time, I take in her appearance. Who dresses up when they work from home? Unless she had a video conference call or a meeting earlier in the day.

"Mrs. Crane, what is it that you do for a living?"

"I'm a psychologist."

"I apologize. I should have been calling you Dr.," I say. "I've never heard of a psychologist who works from home."

"I specialize in helping individuals who have a difficult time leaving their homes. My appointments are done over the phone or through video conferencing."

That would explain her attire. She probably had a video conference with a client today. I wonder how a psychologist would react to my gift of psychometry.

"I'm home," someone calls from the front of the house.

"That's my husband now," Rebecca says, already on her way to greet him.

Dad, Mitchell, and I all exchange a look. Something is odd about Rebecca. I'd love to get another read on her, but I don't think she'll be willing to shake my hand again after our awkward introduction.

Jacob Crane looks to be just as young as his wife. He's wearing a light blue dress shirt and checkered tie with charcoal pants. Rebecca kisses his cheek before he places his briefcase by the door.

"I hope I didn't miss too much," he says, walking over to greet us.

"No, we've only been here for a few minutes," Dad says. "I'm Thomas Ashwell. This is my daughter, Piper, and Detective Brennan from the Weltunkin PD."

"I was hoping you could explain to us why Amelia's case would be reopened after all this time." Jacob takes a seat in the high-backed chair and crosses his hands in his lap.

"You're a psychologist, too," I say, my senses picking up on the fact.

He gives one dip of his head. "I am."

Why on earth would two psychologists think it was okay to allow a seventeen-year-old girl free rein to come and go as she pleases?

"To answer your question," Mitchell says, "we've recently come across new information regarding your niece's case."

"New information?" Rebecca asks, sitting on the arm of her husband's chair. "Such as?"

"That Mr. O'Neil wasn't working alone, and perhaps his partner was actually the one who murdered your niece."

"That's ludicrous," Rebecca says. "Amelia's killer has been in prison for five years. He confessed."

"We believe the arresting officer may have missed a

key piece of evidence, and for that reason, we really need to track down the bird Amelia owned."

"Bird?" Rebecca's eyes widen. "Ms. Ashwell, I can't help but think that you're suffering from some delusion that—"

"She's not suffering from any delusions," Mitchell says. "Piper happens to be psychic."

I want to smack him so hard right now. That was the worst thing he could have said.

"Psychic?" Rebecca starts laughing, and her husband joins in.

"I find it very odd that the two of you are laughing when we're discussing your niece's murder," I say. I move toward a photograph on a small table by the entryway. "You didn't want to take her in, did you? You only did it out of familial obligation. But you wanted her out the second she turned eighteen. That was the deal, right?"

"Wrong." Jacob steeples his fingers in front of his face. "No one forced Amelia to leave. She made that decision on her own, and we supported her need for independence."

These two are as unfeeling as human beings come. My eyes fall on the photograph again. In it, neither Rebecca nor Jacob are dressed the way they are now. They're both wearing jeans and T-shirts. I pick up the photo with my right hand.

"We'll take her in until she turns eighteen. That will give us access to the money my brother left her. We'll get

one of my colleagues to diagnose her with a mental condition and prescribe her medication."

"You want to give her medication for an illness she doesn't have?" Rebecca asks.

"No. It will simply justify the money we remove from her account. We'll give her sugar pills. She'll never know the difference."

I put down the photo. "You lied to her. Told her she had a mental illness so you could get your hands on her money." I'm so disgusted by them that another thought pops into my head. "Did you hire someone to kill her so you could keep her entire inheritance?"

CHAPTER FOUR

The Cranes are both on their feet. "How dare you?" Jacob says. "Get out of my house this instant!" He comes storming over to me as if he's going to physically remove me from his property, but Mitchell is having none of that.

"If you so much as touch her, I will have you in cuffs before you can scream for your lawyer."

Dad takes me by my arm and leads me to the front door. As we step outside, he says, "Don't you think you should have held on to that particular theory until it was just Mitchell, you, and me?"

Quite possibly, but I was too angry to think clearly. I get into the passenger seat of Mitchell's patrol car. One way Dad and I differ is that he's great at controlling his emotions. It's not easy for me, though. Not when I see horrific things in visions.

Mitchell gets in the car and immediately starts the

engine. I'm getting the feeling he wants to get away from the Cranes before he does something foolish, too. "If they really did hire O'Neil..."

"They got one of Jacob's colleagues to diagnose her with some illness and write her a prescription. That's how they stole her money while she was living with them. I'm guessing when she turned eighteen and moved out, she started spending that money and they didn't like it. They wanted the inheritance."

"By the look of their house and clothing, they got it." Mitchell breaks just about every traffic law on the way to my parents' house. He's fuming by the time we arrive.

Mom greets us at the door and holds up her wrist. Tapping her watch, she says, "You're cutting it close." She looks around us. "Where's your father?"

"Probably doing the speed limit. He should be here any minute," I say, stepping inside where Jezebel is sitting, her tail dusting the hardwood floor.

"Hi, my sweet girl," I tell her.

Max takes one look at Jez and then sits.

"Wow," I say. I bend down and pat his head. "Good boy, Max." His tail swishes across the floor, too.

"Go sit and get started before the food gets cold," Mom says. "I'll wait to let your father in."

Mitchell and I head for the dining room, and his eyes light up at the sight of the turkey in the center of the table. Mom didn't carve it yet, so Mitchell grabs the knife and gets to work. By the time he has enough carved to serve everyone, Mom and Dad both join us with the dogs in tow.

Dad's stern expression clues me in to the fact that he's still upset with me. Since I want to eat in peace, I dig right in, scooping stuffed mushrooms onto my plate and then Mitchell's.

"Thanks," Mitchell says, placing three slices of turkey on my plate in return. Our eyes meet, and then he says, "You know, I'm not sure I would have been able to stay so calm if I'd seen what you did. I mean, what kind of monster tries to steal his niece's inheritance right after she lost both parents?"

"What's all this about?" Mom asks, and I'm a little surprised she's showing interest in the case at the moment since she usually tries to ban work talk at the dinner table.

Mitchell dives into a recount of our interaction with the Cranes. I'm thankful he's trying to help smooth things over with Dad, but what really helps is when Mom throws in her two cents.

"So they only took her in to get the inheritance. It makes sense they'd panic when she moved out and took the money with her. I think you're on to something here, Piper."

"Even so," Dad says, "blurting it out that way couldn't have been more counterproductive. I mean, did you really think they'd confess to hiring a hitman?"

No. "I reacted. I know I shouldn't have, but you've

seen what visions can do to me. I take on the emotions of the people I see. They're greedy."

"Which made you want answers right then and there, right?" Mitchell asks.

"Apparently."

Mom reaches for my hand and pats it. "I'm sure it's not easy controlling the emotions like that." Her compassion stems from the fact that her own mother was an empath. Grandma Maywood wound up unable to be around people because experiencing their emotions became too much for her to handle. I'm pretty sure Mom worries more every day that I'll turn out like her mother. It's why she hates that I have so few friends and I never date. It's also the reason why she tries to push Mitchell onto me.

"I'll be fine, Mom. I promise. I'm just sorry I screwed up things for this case. I doubt the Cranes will ever talk to me again." My eyes meet Dad's, and his expression softens.

"I'm sorry, pumpkin. I overreacted back there."

"No, you were right. I should have kept that information to myself until we got here tonight to discuss our next move."

Mitchell looks back and forth between Dad and me, trying to figure out what to say. He doesn't talk to his own father, and while he was close to his brother growing up, they don't speak much now other than obligatory calls on the holidays. He hangs out with us every Tuesday for

Ashwell family dinner night because he likes being around family, but it's still not second nature for him to know how to react in certain situations. "Dinner is delicious, Mrs. Ashwell," he finally says.

"Well, thank you, Mitchell. I know it's nowhere near Thanksgiving, but I was feeling thankful for all the good things in my life and thought a nice turkey dinner would be the perfect thing. I even bought an apple pie for dessert."

"The only thing that could make that any better is if you say you have vanilla ice cream to go on top of the pie."

Mom smiles. "Then I'm about to make your night."

"No way." Mitchell grins like a little kid, and Mom nods.

Dad and I exchange a look. "Did you sense that the Cranes hired a hitman, or were you assuming if they'd fake an illness to steal her money while she lived with them, they'd find a way to get the rest once she'd moved out?"

In truth, I jumped to the conclusion. I don't really want to admit that, though, so I say, "I'm not sure. I'd really like to talk to O'Neil again and get his reaction to my theory."

Mitchell shakes his head. "I don't think it's a good idea to go back to the prison and talk to O'Neil."

"We don't know how to track down Amelia's things. The Cranes certainly aren't going to talk to us anymore." I stab a piece of turkey with my fork.

"Someone else might know," Dad says.

I meet his gaze and realize he's right. "Wonderful."

"What?" Mitchell asks.

"Think about it. Who else knows this case?" I say.

Realization washes over his features. "Andrews."

"Like I said, I'd really prefer working with the convicted felon."

Wednesday morning, Dad, Mitchell, and I show up at the station—a united front against Andrews and the insults I'm sure he's going to sling my way. We're seated at his desk, or rather Mitchell and I are. Dad is standing behind us, arms crossed and looking like the picture of calm.

Officer Gilbert walks in, his eyes zeroing in on Dad, his hero. I suppress a smirk when Officer Andrews walks in behind him and sees the three of us.

"Well, this is not how I want to start my day." He turns to Officer Gilbert. "Get me coffee while I deal with these three."

Officer Gilbert heads toward the conference room, but his gaze remains on Dad, which almost causes him to walk into a wall.

"Damn rookies," Officer Andrews mutters. He still hasn't taken a seat at his desk, and I'm not sure if it's because he doesn't want to have to look up at Dad or if he doesn't want to corner himself in. "What do you three want?"

"We need to find out which charity Amelia Crane's belongings were donated to after she died," I say.

"Ask her family."

"We did."

Officer Andrews laughs. "Let me guess. They didn't want to work with the psychic P.I." He makes air quotes when he says "psychic."

"It was more that they didn't want to talk to me when I discovered they were stealing the inheritance money right out from under Amelia." I bet Officer Andrews never figured that out.

"You have no proof of that." He crosses his arms.

"How much did you look into them?" I ask. "Or did you simply close this case because O'Neil confessed?"

"Let me explain police procedure to you. When someone confesses, you can stop wasting your time searching for the guilty party."

"Unless they're lying."

Officer Andrew's scoffs so loudly he draws the attention of everyone nearby. "You can't possibly think O'Neil didn't kill her."

"I don't think he did. I think he played his part, but someone else killed Amelia." I sit forward in the seat and stare up at Officer Andrews. "Face it. You let a guilty man go free because you were too lazy to look into the case."

Officer Andrews storms off in the direction of the chief's office. The shades are drawn, so I can't even be sure the chief is in.

"I'll talk to Chief Johansen when Andrews comes out," Dad says. "I'll get him to order Andrews to surrender any information he has on the case."

"No. I don't want Officer Andrews's help. We can figure this out on our own." And it's not like we're on a timeline here. Amelia's been dead for years. But the fact that a killer remains free does make me want to find out the truth as soon as possible.

"Let's go." I stand up and walk out, waving to Officer Wallace, whom I pass on his way into the station.

We're in Mitchell's patrol car, about to pull out, when Officer Gilbert runs up to the car and knocks on my window. He looks over his shoulder at the station as I lower the window.

"I know the name of the charity. I worked on the Crane case. Or I studied it. Andrews had me study all his old cases. He said I should learn from the best." Officer Gilbert rolls his eyes, and I swear I like him even more in that moment.

"Anything you could tell us would be great." I look at the doors to see Officer Andrews emerge from the station. "Come by my office later today. I don't want to get you in trouble with your partner. Just tell him Dad left his phone and you ran out here to return it."

Officer Gilbert taps the open window. "Later today," he says before turning and walking away.

"You do realize having him on our side would render Andrews completely useless against us," Mitchell says.

I turn and smile at Dad in the back seat. "I do. And having Officer Gilbert's idol working with me will ensure we always have his cooperation."

We stop at a diner for an actual breakfast since we typically eat a pastry from Marcia's Nook and drink some coffee. All three of us are feeling like feasting this morning. Who knew sticking it to Officer Andrews could muster such an appetite? Mitchell and I both order the breakfast sampler, which has eggs, bacon, sausage, pancakes, and a waffle. Dad opts for a western omelet and shakes his head at Mitchell and me while we do our best to clean our plates. Being able to eat my weight in food is a special talent of mine, and I love to see the looks on people's faces when I do it. No one expects someone as thin as I am to be able to pack away as much food as I can eat in a sitting.

When the waitress comes to take our plates, she looks at Dad and Mitchell as if trying to figure out who helped me eat my food. We all laugh, which makes her uncomfortable. Dad grabs the check for us, and Mitchell leaves the tip. Now that we're all completely stuffed, we head to my office to find out as much as we can about Amelia's parents and how much money they left her. I'm curious to know the price tag for murder. Exactly how much money made Jacob and Rebecca Crane want to hire a hitman to kill their niece?

Carlton and Melissa Crane definitely did well for themselves, considering they were both anesthesiologists.

"Their salaries were huge," Mitchell says. "And they had two of them to live off of."

"Yeah, but there was a catch to Amelia's inheritance," Dad interrupts. "Amelia was only permitted to spend so much on food, clothing, and living arrangements until she turned twenty-five. Then she was free to do whatever she wanted with the money."

"That explains why she lived in a tiny apartment," I say.

Mitchell is standing next to me, reading the laptop screen. "I'm assuming her aunt and uncle had access to the money in order to pay for her living expenses while she was under their roof."

"You got it," Dad says.

"Amelia stood to collect three million dollars on her twenty-fifth birthday," I say. "But it wound up going to her aunt and uncle instead."

"I'd say that gave them plenty of motive to kill her," Mitchell says.

Motive is great and all, but it doesn't solve cases on its own. "Sure, but how do we prove it?"

Dad sighs and turns his chair to face me. "Pumpkin, I'm afraid you're going to have to do as O'Neil said and find Amelia's body."

I hate when cases come down to me reading dead bodies. I'm about to groan when Officer Gilbert walks into my office, and the smile on his face tells me he's about to help this case in a very big way.

CHAPTER FIVE

He looks around the tiny office as if it's the most magnificent place he's ever stepped foot in. I know the reason has everything to do with my father and not my P.I. business, but I don't mind at all. I just need his help.

"Have a seat," I say, motioning to the chair opposite Dad's desk.

"Thank you," Officer Gilbert says, practically beaming at Dad. "This is incredible. I mean, you guys must do amazing things in here."

Does he not realize a lot of what we do is exactly the same as what the Weltunkin PD does, except Dad and I don't carry guns?

"We're glad you could stop by," I say. "You mentioned you know the charity Amelia Crane's belongings were donated to when she was declared dead."

"Yeah. Andrews found out the name of it."

"Why isn't it in the case file then?" Mitchell asks.

"I asked the same question." Officer Gilbert pauses, and for a moment, I think we're going to have to pry every word out of him. Is it Dad's presence that's making him so starstruck, or is there another reason why he's dragging this out?

"Did you get an answer?" Dad asks him.

"Oh, sorry." Officer Gilbert laughs and pats down the front of his uniform shirt. "I have to admit I'm a little distracted. I mean, I've heard all about you both, and I worked that case with Piper and Mitchell, but this is different. Seeing the place where you guys brainstorm and research and... It's just... Well, there are no words."

What is Officer Andrews doing with him if sitting in my office is so exciting for the man?

"How's working with Officer Andrews going?" I ask, knowing I'm getting off topic but hoping to put Officer Gilbert at ease so he'll be more relaxed and able to help us.

"He's..." He shuts his mouth.

I nod. "We know."

Officer Gilbert leans forward in his chair. "Can I be honest with you about something?"

"Of course," I say.

"And it won't get back to Andrews?"

I laugh. "Officer Gilbert, I can assure you I talk to Officer Andrews as little as is humanly possible. I have no desire to change that."

He nods, but then he looks to Dad and Mitchell as if

assessing whether or not they feel the same way I do. When he's finally satisfied, he says, "Okay, well, I thought it was odd that the Crane file was missing so much information. I feel like this case sort of fell in Andrews's lap, and when he got the confession from O'Neil, he just closed it, no questions asked. I mean, O'Neil had no real motive. I don't think he even knew about Amelia's money."

Who would? She lived in a tiny apartment and worked like everyone else. She couldn't flaunt her money if she wanted to because she couldn't touch it until her twenty-fifth birthday.

I look at Officer Gilbert and hold out my right hand. "May I?"

He studies my hand. "May you what exactly?"

"This might be easier if you take my hand and allow me to see the conversation that transpired between you and Officer Andrews. It will also allow you to tell him in good faith that you didn't say anything to me about this case, because you will, in fact, not be telling me anything in your own words."

Officer Gilbert smiles. "Sneaky. So, you can read me? Just by touching my hand?"

"Yup. What do you say?"

Mitchell places his hand on the back of my chair. "You don't have to do a thing. Piper will take care of everything. It's easy, really."

"She's read you?" Officer Gilbert asks, his eyes

volleying between Mitchell and me.

"On more than one occasion," Mitchell says, and out of the corner of my eye, I see Dad's head jerk in my direction. He knows Mitchell thought he had feelings for me. Maybe he still thinks he does. I don't know for sure. And now Dad's questioning if Mitchell let me read him to show just that. He did, and ever since, I've tried my hardest to prove we're better off as friends.

"Piper?" Mitchell says, his hand cupping my shoulder. "You okay?"

I meet his gaze, and he points to Officer Gilbert's hand in mine. Sometimes it's harder for me not to read someone than it is to read them. That's not the case at all right now. I'm holding Officer Gilbert's hand, and I'm not getting anything. "That's odd."

"What do you see?" Officer Gilbert asks.

"Nothing."

"Are your visions blocked?" Dad asks.

"I don't know. Everyone be quiet." I take several deep breaths and close my eyes.

"He wouldn't tell you where the woman's body is? Why confess if you had no real evidence to pin the murder on him?" Officer Gilbert asks.

"He wanted the credit." Officer Andrews leans back in his chair. "I've seen it before."

"Then why not reveal the location of the body?"

"Look, if you want to delve into the mind of a psychotic killer to figure out why he did something, be my guest. I got

a confession. The woman's family is virtually nonexistent and didn't press to find her body, so why should I?"

"And her things? Where did they go?" Officer Gilbert asks.

"Charity. A shelter for troubled teens or something."

I let go of Officer Gilbert's hand. "I'm guessing the shelter for troubled teens was the Hilltop House." It's a huge mansion that was converted into a homeless shelter for teenagers. Jonathon Hill founded the shelter before he died in the late eighties.

"Yeah, that's the one he said. He didn't like me asking questions, though. I think he thought I was questioning his ability to do his job. I got a lecture on respecting senior members of the force." He waves one hand in the air. "I told him I have the utmost respect for Detective Ashwell." Officer Gilbert places both hands on Dad's desk. "I've read about all your cases. I was really hoping to get on the force and learn from you, but..."

But Dad retired a little early and came to work with me. And now poor Officer Gilbert is stuck with Officer Andrews as his partner.

Officer Gilbert stands up. "Well, I should really get going. I'm supposed to be on a lunch run. Do you think Officer Andrews will believe they screwed up the order I called in and I had to wait for it to be remade?"

Lying to his partner? That's not a good start to a relationship where you're supposed to trust each other with your lives. Maybe it's not the best idea for Mitchell and me to be talking to Officer Gilbert like this. He needs to be able to form a good relationship with Officer Andrews. As much as I hate to do it, I say, "Don't be too quick to judge your partner. He knows what he's doing, and I'm sure you'll learn a lot from him."

Dad nods in agreement, but Mitchell is staring at us both like we've lost our minds.

Officer Gilbert says goodbye and rushes out.

"What was that about?" Mitchell asks me.

"I can't have him hating or even distrusting the man he's going to work with every day. You know how dangerous that can turn out to be."

Mitchell looks to Dad, his partner for a very brief time. Mitchell hasn't taken on another partner since, mostly because he views me as his partner even if not in an official WPD capacity.

"All right," Dad says. "Next stop is Hilltop House, right?"

"Right," I say, getting up. "I really need to walk Jez, though."

"What you need to do is drop Jez off with your mother in the mornings. Why did you stop doing that?" Dad stands up.

"I don't know. I guess I should."

"You two go to Hilltop House," Dad says. "I'll go walk Jezebel. I've been meaning to stop in to see Theodore anyway."

I kiss his cheek. "Thanks, Dad."

Mitchell holds the door open for me. "Do you think Hilltop really kept the bird around? If there ever was a bird, that is."

I get in the passenger seat of the patrol car. "There's a bird. O'Neil wouldn't have mentioned one if there wasn't."

Mitchell starts the engine and pulls out of the lot. "Unless I was right and the bird meant jailbird."

He could have been talking about himself, but ever since I saw the birdcage, I've known I need to read it. It holds answers to this case. I'm sure of it. "Hopefully, we'll find out soon enough."

Hilltop House is run by Theresa Hill, Jonathon Hill's granddaughter. She's a pretty woman in her mid-forties with auburn hair and blue eyes. She's dressed in black pants and a pink blouse, and her perfume reminds me of lilacs. I really hate perfume since my sense of smell is heightened. It tends to make me sneeze.

Mitchell flashes his badge and his pearly whites at Theresa, which must flatter her because she starts batting her eyes at him and acting much younger than her age.

She welcomes us inside and immediately loops her arm through Mitchell's. For some unknown reason, her flirting is irritating me. And when she comments on his firm biceps, I can't take it anymore.

"Mrs. Hill—"

"*Ms.* Hill," she corrects me, giving Mitchell a smile in the process.

"Sorry, I just assumed a woman of your age would be married by now."

Mitchell's eyes widen at me, and then he smirks. "I think Piper meant to say a woman of your beauty."

I most certainly did not mean to say that. Still, Mitchell's compliment seems to appease her. "We need to know if you have the ornate bird cage that belonged to Amelia Crane. It was supposed to have been donated here five years ago after she was murdered."

"Oh, I remember that case. It was all over the news. That man who killed her showed no remorse."

Probably because he didn't actually kill her.

"He was attractive, though. I remember seeing his face on the television and thinking it must have been easy for him to lure that young woman somewhere private. His eyes were the most beautiful shade of blue. Much like yours, Detective."

"Mitchell's eyes are green. Green, not blue." God, what is wrong with me?

Mitchell cocks his head at me. "Some days they look almost turquoise, which is a blue-green, so I can see the confusion."

"Is the bird cage still here?" I ask, crossing my arms.

"Yes. It's in the library upstairs." She motions toward the stairs, and I follow the two of them up.

I'm finding it odd that I haven't seen any teenage girls around even though this is supposed to be a shelter for them. "Where are the other residents?" I ask.

"We have a teacher come every day to homeschool the girls. They're in the study."

A study and a library. Not bad. I have to say Jonathon Hill had a great thing going with this place. I admire him for putting his money to such good use.

Theresa brings one finger to her lips as we pass by a door that's partially closed over. I can hear a woman talking about the Civil War, so I assume that's the study where the homeschooling is taking place.

Theresa opens the door at the end of the hallway. "In here," she whispers, winking at Mitchell.

Seriously? She has about fifteen years on him. She can't possibly think he'd be interested in her.

Oh, no. I stop in the doorway, staring at the two of them, and realize what the problem is. I'm jealous. This can *not* be happening. I'm just coming to terms with being Mitchell's friend. There is no way I can possibly have feelings beyond friendship for the man. It would never work.

Yet earlier today I touched Officer Gilbert's hand without reading him. Maybe with my abilities expanding, I'm gaining better control over them, too. Maybe I can...

"Piper?" Mitchell is about two feet in front of me. His hands grip my arms. "You look like you've seen a ghost. Did you have a vision?"

Sort of. But it was more like a glimpse of a semi-normal life for me.

"No," I say. "Sorry."

"Why are you always apologizing?" He squeezes my arms and then lowers his hands so they're holding mine.

My entire body tenses, and I beg myself not to read him.

He lets go. "Sorry. After earlier in your office with Gilbert, I thought maybe you got control over that."

"I think I might have. At least a little."

He smiles. "You looked absolutely petrified."

Because I was. I don't know what this means for me. Or what it means that I'm jealous of a woman I know Mitchell is only tolerating because she's helping us with this case. I don't know how to handle anything I'm feeling right now, and it's making me lightheaded, which is the worst possible thing considering I'm going to need to read that bird cage.

"Detective," Theresa calls.

Mitchell's eyes are locked on mine. "I've got to go play nice so you can have a vision in peace. Wish me luck. This one is feisty."

I force a brief laugh and watch him walk over to Theresa, who is standing next to the bird cage. There is a bird inside. A smaller bird than I would have guessed, but I suppose that would explain why Amelia was blocking the bird in the photograph. It's yellow with an orange oval on its cheek. Do birds have cheeks? And it has a plume on its head.

"What kind of bird is that?" I ask, since I know exactly nothing about birds.

"A cockatiel. We debated turning the bird over to an animal shelter, but the girls enjoy talking to it and feeding it." Theresa moves closer to the cage. "This cage is quite expensive, too. It's an antique."

I'm tempted to ask if the bird will bite me if I touch the cage, since I'm definitely going to have to touch the cage to read it, but Theresa is already deep in conversation with Mitchell again.

He meets my gaze for a brief moment before placing his hand on Theresa's elbow and gently directing her away from me. I know he's giving me privacy, but I still don't like it. God, what is wrong with me?

I shake the thoughts from my mind and focus on the cage. The bird chirps a few times and then starts eating from the dish inside the cage. I figure this is the perfect time to have a vision since even the bird is preoccupied.

I place my right hand on the cage.

Amelia rushes into the apartment, locking the door behind her. She looks through the peephole and then presses her back against the door. "Am I crazy, Jeffrey?"

The cockatiel whistles in response, and Amelia laughs, but it's a nervous laugh.

"I saw him again. The same man. It's like he's everywhere I go. Him and his blue eyes.

CHAPTER SIX

The vision ends, and I let go of the cage just as Jeffrey comes over to inspect my hand. I pull away in case he's a biter.

Mitchell moves to my side. "Everything okay?"

"Yeah. Ms. Hill, you said the bird cage is expensive?"

"Very. Why?"

I need to be able to read this thing more, and I don't want to come back here and have to deal with her throwing herself at Mitchell again.

Mitchell must sense where I'm going with this because he says, "This cage is crucial to our investigation." He moves toward her and drops his voice, "Any chance you'd be willing to let me borrow it for a few days?"

"Borrow the bird or the cage?" she asks.

I'd prefer just the cage, but O'Neil's comment about

the bird comes to mind, and I blurt out, "Both. Mitchell's been talking about getting a pet, and this would be a great trial run for him as well."

He eyes me suspiciously, but says, "Yeah, it would." He turns back to Theresa. "It would really mean a lot to me, and I assure you I'd take very good care of—"

"Jeffrey," I say.

Theresa laughs, placing her palm to her chest as if I've just said the funniest thing ever. "Jeffrey? What kind of a name is that for a bird? His name is Tweety."

I roll my eyes. She thinks giving the bird a human name is crazy, but naming it after a cartoon character is perfectly acceptable?

"It would mean a great deal to me," Mitchell says, and Theresa practically melts into the floor.

I turn away, not wanting to witness this anymore. I'm not sure how we'd even get this cage to his place, but before I can figure that out, Theresa is beside me, saying, "The top unscrews from the base. Detective, if you'd be so kind as to use those muscles to lift the cage, I'll unscrew the bottom."

"Certainly. Thank you," Mitchell says, carefully lifting the cage so as not to disturb Jeffrey.

"Oh my. You are strong," Theresa says, and she begins using both hands to unscrew the base of the cage.

Ten agonizingly long minutes later, we're back inside the patrol car. The top of the cage is secured in the back seat, and the base is lying across the floor back there as well.

"That went well," Mitchell says, turning to smile at me as he starts the engine.

"Maybe from your perspective, but my view was practically vomit-inducing."

He laughs. "Well, I can see why." He stares at me. "I think you know why, too, but until you're ready to admit you have feelings for me—"

"Yeah, feelings of..." Every insult I've ever given him seems to have evaded my thoughts.

"It's okay. You're not ready. I get it." He pulls out of the driveway and back onto the road.

Damn him. Now I'm going to have to look at his smug face for the rest of the day because I can't even deny his claim.

"We could play the game if you'd like."

The game is something we use a lot on cases. I clear my mind, and Mitchell asks me a series of questions. The answers just sort of pop into my head, which gives us leads. "For what purpose?" I ask. "It's not like I have a clue in this case that we're trying to figure out."

"In the O'Neil case, no. But in the case of Ashwell vs. Brennan we do."

"No, we do not. There's no case there whatsoever. I've admitted you're my best friend. I'm still dealing with the consequences. Give me time to get used to it. It's left me somewhat flustered."

He flashes another smile at me. "Oh, it has you flustered all right. I saw the way you reacted to Theresa Hill back there. In a word, you were jealous."

"Jealous?" I scoff. "Please."

"Are you saying you liked the way she was flirting with me?"

"No, it was disgusting."

"So, it bothered you."

"Well, yeah. She's...older."

"Did it bother you for any other reason?"

"She was throwing herself at you."

"And you didn't like that?"

"Of course not."

"Because you hate it when women flirt with me."

"Yeah."

"Because you like me."

His question snaps me to attention. "I can't believe you just did that."

He bobs one shoulder but won't look at me. "Did what?"

"You were playing the game, and making me play it without even realizing it." It almost worked too, but his last question surprised me so much I stopped myself from answering. I'm not ready to answer it. Not to him or to myself.

"I'm sorry. I shouldn't have done that to you. It wasn't fair." He looks at me for a brief moment, and I can see the sadness in his eyes. "I just wish you'd be straight with me,

Piper. Partners really do have to trust each other completely. That means no secrets. I shared my secret with you, and believe me when I say it wasn't easy to do."

"But you said we were better this way. That being friends was what's best for us." He lied to me. Just like I lied about having a vision of us breaking up and it destroying our ability to work together.

"I'm sorry for that, too. I didn't know what else to do to make you keep being my partner and not act all"—he removes his right hand from the wheel and gestures to me —"Piper-ish around me."

"Piper-ish is not a word."

"What can I say? There really aren't adequate words to describe you."

I look out the passenger window, mostly to avoid Mitchell's gaze. Neither of us talks for about five minutes. And then Mitchell finally breaks the silence.

"I like you, Piper. A lot. You can do with that what you will. It's up to you. I wasn't lying when I said I'm okay with us. If this is what you want and what you feel you can handle, I'll deal with that." He reaches over and takes my left hand in his. "But I'm okay with this, too."

I look down at our hands and blink back the tears threatening to betray my true feelings. I do have feelings for Mitchell, but I don't know how to deal with them. I don't know how to do this, and I'm nothing like the women he dates.

I pull my hand away and slide it under my leg so he

can't try holding it again. "I can't be who you want me to be. I'm not like those other women."

"Who said I wanted you to be like them?" He pulls up in front of his condo and cuts the engine. Turning in his seat, he says, "Piper, look at me."

I meet his gaze but slide closer to the door to keep distance between us.

"I have a confession. I've been lying about dating, too."

I shake my head. "I've read you. I saw you with—"

He holds up a hand to stop me. "That was when we first started working together. I really haven't dated anyone since. When I said I did, that was a lie. One I told to try to make you more comfortable around me. The truth is that's not who I want to be anymore. I've never fit into anyone's life the way I fit into yours. You can't deny I practically live at your place now. I come here to change my clothes."

God, how did I let this happen?

His gaze locks on mine. "You push my buttons, and you challenge me every step of the way, but damn it, I've never felt so comfortable with anyone."

He just expressed exactly how I feel about him. I reach my left hand out and place it on his forearm. "I know. Same here. I just..."

"You need time to adjust." He nods. "Okay. I'm going to stop pretending to see other women, though, okay? Do you know what it was like trying to flirt with that blonde from your apartment complex in case you read Jez?"

"You did that to fool me?"

"I knew you'd read her to spy on me."

"Fair enough." I look down at my hand, which is still on his arm. "What do you say we get this bird cage back together and find a dead body?"

"Nothing I'd rather do," he says with a smile.

"I thought you said no more lying," I tease, opening my door.

He grabs my left hand and stares into my eyes. "I meant nothing I'd rather do than be with you, and that's the truth, Piper."

I lower my eyes before I do something really stupid. "Let's get to work then," I say, forcing a smile on my face as I step out of the car, which feels like it's suffocating me. I take a few deep breaths before opening the back door and grabbing the base of the cage.

Mitchell grabs the other half of the bird cage, and we head inside. Mitchell's done nothing to furnish the place since I was last here. The living room still consists of a couch and one chair. And the only thing on the walls is the large screen TV mounted above the fireplace. The coffee table is covered in a thick layer of dust, but I can still make out the watermarks from him never using a coaster.

Mitchell puts the top of the bird cage down on the floor beside the coffee table. "Sorry, I haven't cleaned in a while. Is the dust going to kill your senses?" he asks, opening a small door in the front entryway. He reaches inside and comes out with a duster.

I laugh. "Do you have a maid uniform to go with that feather duster, Detective?"

"Wouldn't you like to know?" He smiles at me and immediately starts dusting the table. "I have one of those robotic vacuums, so at least the floor is clean."

I put the base of the bird cage in the corner by the couch. "Is here okay?"

"Sure." Mitchell grabs the top half of the cage, and I screw in the base.

"There," I say. "So, Jeffrey—not Tweety—witnessed Amelia coming home to her apartment after swearing she was followed by someone with piercing blue eyes."

"Blue? Like O'Neil's?" Mitchell asks. "Do you think he lied to us?"

"I don't know." My senses can work like lie detectors, but they didn't pick up any deceit from O'Neil in that prison. Still, it's happened before, so I won't rule out the possibility that O'Neil hid information from me.

I reach for the cage.

"Who are you? How did you get my number?" Amelia says into the phone. Her one hand is raised to her mouth, and she's biting on her thumbnail.

"You need to listen to me if you want to live. Don't go to the theater tonight."

"Are you threatening me?"

"I'm trying to save your life. If you go to the theater tonight, he will be there, and he will kill you."

"Who?"

An audible click on the other end of the line ends the call.

I open my eyes and turn to Mitchell. "I can't believe it."

"What? What did you see?"

"It was O'Neil, the man with the blue eyes, but I don't think he was following her because he intended to harm her." I meet Mitchell's gaze. "I think he was trying to stop someone else from hurting her."

"Are you saying he went to jail for a crime he didn't commit? He wasn't involved in Amelia's murder at all?"

"He tried to save her."

"From who?"

I shake my head. "I don't know."

Mitchell runs his hand over the scruff on his chin. "We have to go back to the prison to talk to O'Neil, don't we?"

"Before it's too late," I say without knowing why.

"What?" Mitchell asks. "Are you sensing something?"

I raise my hand to my mouth as I realize what my senses must be trying to tell me. "O'Neil went to jail to avoid being killed by the same man who killed Amelia. He figured he'd be safe there. But now that he's contacted us, he's not safe anymore."

"Are you saying the killer knows he talked to us?"

"Yes," I answer, knowing it's true.

"Damn it." Mitchell consults his watch. "Visiting

hours are over for the day. We'll have to wait until tomorrow."

"Tomorrow will be too late," I say. "You need to pull some strings and get us in there now. Or he'll be dead by morning."

CHAPTER SEVEN

Now that I've had a few premonitions, I can usually recognize when the information I'm getting is coming from the future. In this case, I'm sensing immediate danger around O'Neil. It hasn't happened yet, though. It's foggy inside my head. Just out of reach but near.

Mitchell's phone is to his ear. "This is Detective Brennan with the Weltunkin PD. I have reason to believe one of your inmates, Levi O'Neil, is in danger. I need to speak with him immediately." He pauses. "I'll have the chief call you if need be, but this is a matter of life and death." Another pause. "Fine. I'll be there in fifteen minutes." He hangs up. "They're going to move him to solitary until we get there."

Mitchell takes a step toward me. "Piper, how could this guy get to O'Neil in prison? It doesn't make sense."

Unless this man is someone who works at the prison.

A guard, maybe. Or he could be another inmate. None of these thoughts are giving me a definite yes on my radar. "I don't know, Mitchell. I just know he's in danger."

He nods, and we rush out of the condo.

On the drive, Mitchell calls Chief Johansen to fill him in. He doesn't mention anything about this being a possible inside job, because it would be career suicide to make an implication like that with absolutely no concrete evidence. Not to mention if I'm wrong, Chief Johansen would put an end to Mitchell using me as a consultant on any future cases.

I call Dad and tell him what's going on, and he has his own theory.

"Pumpkin, you have to consider the possibility that the real murderer has connections inside that prison."

"You mean like another inmate," I say.

"Exactly. If they're communicating, the killer could easily put a hit on O'Neil without going anywhere near him." He's right. And if this guy is as scary as O'Neil's led me to believe, then he can probably bully any convict into doing his bidding.

"Thanks, Dad. Do me a favor and stay away from this one, okay?" I can't handle the thought of Dad getting hurt on another one of my cases.

"You do realize I'm your father. I'm supposed to say things like that to you, not the other way around."

"Who do you think I learned this from?" I ask.

"Tell you what. I'll agree to this on one condition."

Mitchell disconnects from his call and turns to look at me. I put my phone on speaker so he can hear.

"You stick with Mitchell. I mean all the time, until this case is closed. Have one of those sleepovers of yours."

Mitchell laughs. "Will do, sir."

"They aren't sleepovers," I say, shaking my head at both of them. "But fine. Mitchell can sleep on my couch."

"No can do," Mitchell says. "I'm bird sitting, remember?"

I forgot. "Dad, can you grab Jez and keep her at your place until we're finished with this case?"

"Consider it done. Max has never been so well-behaved. Jezebel is actually teaching him right from wrong."

"She is pretty incredible that way. Tell her I love her and I'll miss her terribly."

Dad doesn't protest because we all know Jez is incredibly smart and will probably understand every word of that. "Will do, pumpkin. Keep me informed, okay?"

"You got it. Thanks, Dad." I hang up.

"So, you're sleeping over at my place this time."

"It's not a sleepover," I say. "We're working."

"My couch sucks, so you'll have to take my room."

"No way."

"I just bought a new mattress, and seeing as I sleep on your couch more than in my own bed, it's only been slept on a few times. The sheets are clean, too."

I wave a hand in the air. "Let's just focus on O'Neil. I

need to talk to him without a glass partition between us. Think you can make that happen?"

"I do. I take it your plan is to read him so he doesn't have to implicate anyone."

"Exactly, although I don't think that will be enough. The damage is already done. The killer knows O'Neil talked to me. He's going after him now anyway."

"Chief Johansen said he'll pull some strings to get maximum protection for O'Neil. He's now being considered a witness to a murder. Chief wants this guy to be caught. He doesn't care how, and he's more than willing to use O'Neil to do it."

And to use me. He knew I'd be in danger taking on this case, too. "If this guy does get to O'Neil, he'll come after me next."

The car jerks to the right as Mitchell whips his head in my direction.

"Whoa!" I say, grabbing the door handle. "Easy there. Don't go helping this lunatic by offing me in this car."

"Sorry, but did you get the sense you're next on this guy's hit list?"

"Not in a psychic vision kind of way, but it only makes sense. He wants to get rid of everyone who knows he's guilty. That's O'Neil and now me."

"And me," Mitchell says, turning onto the road where the prison is located.

Something feels wrong about that. "You aren't

psychic. You can't prove O'Neil isn't the one who killed Amelia Crane. Only I can."

"I'm a police detective. I can figure this out."

"No, you can't. He covered his tracks too well. He pinned this on O'Neil, and the only other person who knows for sure that O'Neil didn't do it is dead. That just leaves me."

Mitchell pulls up to the security station and flashes his badge. The guard checks his list, which has Mitchell's name on it thanks to Chief Johansen, and then raises the gate to let us in.

As soon as we park, Mitchell turns to me. "Like your dad said, you don't leave my sight. Got it? None of your stunts, Piper. I'm not losing you."

I can't deny there's a part of me that wants to keep Mitchell out of this, but there's the other part that doesn't want to do this without him. "Partners stick together, right?"

He squeezes my left hand. "Right."

We get out of the car, and Mitchell brings us in through a different entrance. This one is for the guards. He flashes his badge, and after a few words to the guard, we're brought to an interrogation room. I stare at the two-way mirror, wondering who is on the other side watching our interaction with O'Neil. It makes me question if maybe the killer is someone who works here rather than an inmate, but I really can't say for sure. What I can do is say something in this interview that will let me figure out down the road if this is an inside job.

A few minutes later, O'Neil is brought in, his hands cuffed. The guard attaches those cuffs to a metal ring on the table once O'Neil is seated across from us. O'Neil waits until the guard leaves before he starts talking.

"You shouldn't have come back."

"I believe you're in danger here," I say. "Even though you chose to go to prison for a crime you didn't commit—a crime you actually tried to prevent—you have a target on your head because you talked to me."

"Did you see that?" he asks me.

I decide to take a huge risk here and play the psychic card in my hand. "I saw us protecting you. We'll make sure you're safe. There's no reason for anyone to kill you when you've told us exactly nothing. I'm the one who figured this out."

"You found the bird. How is Jeffrey?" O'Neil asks.

"How well did you know Amelia?" Mitchell asks him.

"I followed her for about two months. I knew where she worked, where she lived, that she had a pet bird." O'Neil shrugs. "I was inside her apartment once. I should have taken her. I should have carried her out of there and gotten her away from him. That's how they convicted me, you know. My prints were at her place."

All because he tried to save her. "Why were you there if not to get her away from the killer?"

"I was trying to scare her into leaving on her own. I

ransacked the place. I didn't touch the bird, though. I'd never hurt a living creature." He pauses and takes a deep breath. "He can talk, you know. That's how I know his name. He said 'Jeffrey wants a cracker.'" O'Neil laughs, but it's sad. "I gave him one, too. And I told the damn bird my name."

Something comes to me as soon as he says it. "The bird named you to the police."

O'Neil nods. "After I confessed, they checked her apartment, found my prints, and while they were searching, the damn bird says, 'O'Neil.' Can you believe that?"

I sit forward, intent on reaching for his hand and reading him, but as soon as O'Neil realizes what I'm trying to do, he starts yelling.

"Don't touch me! Someone get me out of here. Don't let her touch me!"

I sit back in my seat, and Mitchell puts his arm out in front of me, to protect me from I don't know what.

The guard comes in and takes O'Neil out of the room.

"We can't just let him go," I say. I drop my voice to a whisper so only Mitchell can hear me, just in case anyone is on the other side of the two-way mirror. "He isn't safe here."

O'Neil is terrified, and I realize coming here only made things worse for him.

"Mitchell, if he dies, it will be my fault."

Mitchell grabs my left hand. "Come on." He pulls me from the room, and we approach the first guard we see.

"Where is O'Neil being taken?" he asks the guard.

"We were told to keep him in solitary until we're informed otherwise."

He'll be away from other prisoners but not the guards, and right now, I'm not sure if that will be enough to keep him alive. I don't know how to protect him.

Then I get a crazy idea. "Can we have him transferred?" I ask Mitchell.

"*We* can't, but we could put in a request with the chief. A transfer will take time, though."

Something we don't have. "I can't leave here knowing it could be the last time we see him. I need to read him, but if he won't let me, I need to make sure no one can get to him." I don't know where he is or who is with him. I don't like any of this.

"Maybe I can get us permission to do rounds with the guards," Mitchell says. "It will put us in contact with the inmates, and you might get a read off one of them."

He wants me to sense a killer in a prison full of killers? I don't bother pointing out how absurd that is. "Give me a list of names. Every inmate, guard, and staff member here."

"You got it." Mitchell leads me to an office, and while he talks to someone about getting the information I need, I stare at the empty visitation room. They've tried to paint this place so it doesn't look so gloomy. There are colorful murals on the walls. I have to think it's meant to benefit the families of inmates more than anything else. I certainly couldn't imagine visiting a family member in here.

A guard walks by, his eyes on me as if he recognizes me. He pauses and then heads in my direction. I'm sure he's going to ask for my ID or for the reason I'm here today when visiting hours are over. He can't see Mitchell inside the office from his angle. But as soon as he reaches me, he wags a finger at me and says, "You're that psychic P.I., aren't you?"

I can't resist. "And you're that prison guard, aren't you?"

His head jerks back a bit. "You've heard of me?"

"Not even a little bit. Sorry. It's just odd when people recognize me for what I do and not my name."

"Sorry, I didn't even think you might take offense to that." He seems nice enough. "Your name starts with an A, right?"

"Ashwell. Piper Ashwell."

"Yeah, that's it. Your father was a police detective, too. I guess it runs in the family, huh?"

"I guess it does." My psychic abilities run in the family too, but I don't volunteer that information.

"So, what brings you here today?"

"A case I'm working on alongside the Weltunkin PD." I jerk a thumb over my shoulder at Mitchell in the office.

"Anything I could be of help with?" he asks, and the expression on his face tells me the offer is genuine.

"That depends on how well you know Levi O'Neil," I say.

"O'Neil." He nods. "He's the quiet type. Keeps to himself. Out of everyone here, he might be the one who actually feels guilty for the crime he committed."

Except I'm not sure he did commit a crime. Well, other than perjury. He did lie about murdering Amelia Crane. "Does he hang out with anyone in particular?"

It's possible the real killer already has someone on the inside sticking close to O'Neil to make sure he stays quiet.

"Not really. He eats by himself and works out by himself. I don't really see him interact with anyone but the guards."

The guards. That leads me to my next question. "Is there a guard he interacts with more than others?" It dawns on me that I still don't know this guard's name. "I'm so sorry. How rude of me? I didn't even ask your name."

"Hancock, and before you ask, there's no relation to John."

I laugh. "Duly noted." I wait for him to answer my other question. The one I really need to know the answer to.

"Let me think. The guard who talks to O'Neil the most is probably Spencer."

"Does he happen to be here now?" I ask, since I'm not getting any initial reaction to the guard's name.

"He should be. Let me check." He gets on his radio. "Spencer, what's your location?"

"Spencer went home sick about thirty minutes ago," a voice says in response.

Thirty minutes ago? That was about the time Mitchell and I showed up. That strikes me as more than a little interesting.

"You ready?" Mitchell says, coming up behind me and making me jump.

"Hang on." I grab the list of names from him and flip through to the sheet that displays all the guards' names. "Hugo Spencer," I say as it practically jumps off the page at me. "Bingo!"

CHAPTER EIGHT

Mitchell and I are out of the prison as fast as possible. It's getting late and we're both starving, but we have a lead. I pull up Hugo Spencer's home address while Mitchell drives with his lights on to get us there faster. The fact that Spencer left when Mitchell and I got to the prison makes him look guilty. And the fact that my senses immediately zeroed in on his name only solidifies it in both our minds.

"If we're dealing with a crooked prison guard, this is going to get ugly," Mitchell says. "I should probably call the chief and fill him in."

No. "My senses are telling me to hold off on calling the chief."

Mitchell gives me the side-eye. "Do you realize how much trouble I could get in for that? He specifically told me to keep him updated on this case."

"I know, but I feel like we need to wait. Like you said, this could be huge."

"Exactly, Piper. It could be huge, and if I don't make sure the chief hears about it first, he's going to have my ass."

"What if we're wrong?" I look down at my lap. "I've misinterpreted visions before. I've had people's names pop out at me for the wrong reasons before, too." I'm not ready to jump the gun on something this big. "The implications are too huge to be wrong. I can't be the psychic who cried wolf." It could cost me all my future cases with the WPD.

"Okay."

I expected more of a fight. "Really? Just like that?"

"If I'm being honest, it really pisses me off that I never heard from the chief when I worked with your dad."

"You mean on the one case you worked with my dad?" I tease him.

"You know what I mean, Piper. You didn't even meet the man until just recently. Why is he suddenly poking his nose into my cases?"

"Because someone told him he should," I say without thinking.

Mitchell's gaze meets mine. "Truth?"

I nod, and he focuses on the road again.

"Andrews," Mitchell says. "It has to be him."

"I agree, and that means Chief Johansen isn't keeping tabs on *you*. He's after me." Officer Andrews is trying to get rid of me after I made him look stupid on the previous case. "Damn him. I even let him take credit with that woman's family and act like he was the one who found her body after all this time."

"I think it's the *after all this time* part that was the problem. He was the officer who failed to solve her case in the first place. Even if he had been the one to find her—which he wasn't—it took five years. Not exactly impressive by any means."

"Then he should have listened to me and helped us on that case."

"Agreed, but neither of us is going to change him or make him see reason. So, what do we do about this case and Chief Johansen?" He glances my way again.

"We solve this case and make the chief see how petty Officer Andrews was being going to him about me in the first place." Officer Andrews is going to find out that I don't back down from a challenge. Only one of us is going to come out of this looking good, and I plan for that person to be me.

Hugo Spencer lives in a gated community, which means we have to provide our names to the security guard, who then calls Hugo to ask if he wants to let us in. Mitchell's badge won't do us any good since we have no reason other than my psychic abilities to suspect Mr. Spencer is guilty of anything.

"I'm sorry, but Mr. Spencer is ill and isn't taking guests at the current time," the security guard tells Michell, handing him back his license.

I realize Hugo wouldn't be denying our visit unless he, like Hancock, has heard of me and believes I really do have psychic abilities. I lean over the middle console to look the security guard in the eyes. "If you wouldn't mind calling Mr. Spencer back and telling him Piper Ashwell, the psychic private investigator, has a very important message for him that he needs to hear right now, I think he'll allow us to drop by for a minute or two."

The guard shakes his head, but he makes the call. Nonbelievers can be so frustrating to deal with. He could have at least kept his thoughts to himself until we pulled away. He's just lucky I can't reach him from here, or I just might "accidentally" come in contact with him and find out what kind of secrets he's hiding.

He hangs up the phone. "All right. Mr. Spencer says you can pass." He rolls his eyes in disbelief as he opens the gate for us.

I give him a smug smile, hoping it pisses him off as much as his head shaking and eye rolling is angering me.

Mitchell follows his GPS through the community, which is on a golf course. "This place is nice." The streetlights illuminate the edges of the course, which looks pristine. "What's the very important message you have for Hugo?" He takes the next right.

"No idea. I'm hoping I can get a read on him right away, and then I'll actually have something to relay to him." Of course, if he's guilty, he's not going to like it one bit.

"You're thinking he believes in what you do?" Mitchell asks.

"At least to a certain degree. Why else would he agree to hear my message?"

"True, but if it was my presence at the prison that made him run off and he really isn't guilty of what we're thinking, he might want your help in proving that."

Which I'll be happy to do if it's true. "I guess we'll find out soon. How close are we?" I ask, looking at the GPS screen.

"That house right there," Mitchell says as we approach a large white house with two balconies and a water fountain out front. "Hmm, I guess prison guards make more money than I realized."

"Yeah, I don't think so," I say. Considering who they have to babysit on a daily basis, they are severely underpaid in my mind. "The money is his wife's," I blurt out.

Mitchell pulls into the driveway and cuts the engine. "Your abilities are getting incredibly good."

"Thanks," I say as I unclick my seat belt. "It would be better if they'd just point me to the real killer so we can close this case, though."

"Wouldn't that be nice? I think that's asking for too much from yourself."

"When don't I?" I step out of the car, and Mitchell falls into step with me as we approach the front door.

"Since I was the one who got us the invite, I think you should let me steer the conversation."

He gestures to the door. "Be my guest."

I raise my hand to press the doorbell.

"Did you just do that without reading it?" he asks.

I nod. "I was purposely tuning out. I'd rather read Hugo himself," I say in a hushed voice as the sound of footsteps on the other side of the door gets closer.

When the door opens, a short man with thinning hair and a goatee stands in front of me. "I thought you'd be taller," he says to me.

I'm five-four, so I'm not tall by any means, but I don't think I'm all that short either. He, on the other hand, barely looks to have an inch on me. I refrain from telling him I expected him to be taller as well. It's not really the first impression I want to make. Instead, I extend my right hand to him while clearing my mind. "Piper Ashwell. Nice to meet you, Mr. Spencer."

The second his hand touches mine, I close my eyes.

Hugo's eyes widen when he reads the visitation log. "Piper Ashwell is here? As in the psychic P.I.?"

"Yeah, pretty cool, huh?" Hancock says. "I hope I run into her."

"Yeah." Hugo's gaze goes back to the log to check the inmate's name. He looks up to see Hancock is already gone. "Fitzpatrick, what's O'Neil being questioned for?"

Fitzpatrick is the guard sitting at the sign-in desk. "Not sure. Some case the WPD is working on."

"I've got to get out of here before they find out I've been helping him," Hugo thinks before faking a cough and rubbing his throat. "I think I caught whatever Aston had earlier in the week. I should really get out of here before I get anyone else sick and there's no one to keep these criminals in line."

Hugo tugs his hand from mine. "What did you do?" he asks, looking at me like I just robbed a bank.

"Mr. Spencer, you left the prison because you were afraid I'd find out you've been helping someone. Who exactly?"

He holds up both hands in front of him. "I don't know what you're talking about. I left because I'm sick."

"You look fine to me," Mitchell says.

Hugo coughs into his fist. "Something's going around the prison. I think I caught it early enough, though. I took medicine."

"You don't know what it is that's going around, but you were able to take medicine for it?" I ask. "Interesting. Almost as interesting as who it is you don't want me to know you're helping."

"I told you I don't know what you're talking about." He starts to close the door, but Mitchell sticks out his boot to block it. "Hey," Hugo says. "You have no right to come here and question me like this."

"You invited us," I say, trying to figure out why he'd run from me and then invite me here. "Wait a minute. You left the prison in hopes that I wouldn't find out something, but when we showed up at the gate and wouldn't leave, you decided I could help you. So why aren't you asking me for help?"

Mitchell furrows his brow at me, not following.

"I know you're helping someone, but it's not who I was thinking. It's O'Neil."

Hugo stops pushing on the door and leans his head on it instead. "Look, the guy isn't like the others. He acts like an average guy. If I didn't know he'd murdered someone, I'd say he was a good man."

"What if he didn't murder anyone?" I ask.

Hugo narrows his eyes at me. "He confessed. I think he wishes he never did it, and that's what makes him different from the others. They all just wish they didn't get caught, but they're fine with having committed the crimes."

"Except, I'm not sure O'Neil did commit a crime. I think he might have been in the wrong place at the wrong time." The only way I'm going to get Hugo to talk to me is if I tell him what I know. Show him that I'm trying to help O'Neil just like he is. "I had a vision of the woman O'Neil supposedly killed. She thought he was stalking her, but I think he was actually trying to save her life."

Hugo runs a hand over his balding head. "That would actually make a lot of sense."

Good. Now we might get somewhere with this guy.

"Can we come in and talk?" Mitchell asks. It's not

exactly cold this evening, but discussing murder on a front porch in the dark like this does feel more than a little odd.

"Yeah, I guess so. I mean if you're really trying to help prove O'Neil's innocence, then I'd like to help." He steps aside to let us in.

"Thank you," I say as I walk into his house.

Mitchell takes in the interior. "Is your wife home?" he asks Hugo.

"No, she's a surgeon. She keeps crazy hours." Hugo motions to the living room. "Please, have a seat."

The room is white. Like all white. White leather couch. White chairs. White fireplace and mantel. White throw rugs. Maybe the surgeon is obsessed with things being clean.

A soft knock on the door makes Hugo turn around. "That's probably one of the security guards checking up after I denied your visit at first. They're pretty great like that. Give me one second. Please, make yourselves at home."

He leaves the room, and I walk over to the fireplace mantel. There are several pictures—in white frames—of Hugo and his wife. She's a petite woman with very dark hair, or maybe it just looks really dark in comparison to the all-white outfit she's wearing in every photo.

A muffled gunshot followed by a thud draws my attention back to the door. Mitchell has his own gun unholstered and poised in front of him.

"Piper, stay where you are," he says in the firmest

voice I've ever heard him use as he moves toward the front door.

I have no intention of moving because I know what that sound was. Someone just shot the one person other than O'Neil who might have been able to help Mitchell and me solve this case.

CHAPTER NINE

Mitchell hands me the mug of tea. "It's ridiculous that you're insisting on sleeping on the couch."

"I refuse to stay here otherwise," I say. There's no way I'm kicking him out of his bed. More than that, there is no way I'm getting into his bed, where I could read so much more than I ever wanted to.

"I'm not going to argue with you. It's late, and I'm beat." He sits down beside me on the couch. "Did you call your dad to check in?"

"Yeah, while you were making tea. Jez is fine."

"What did your dad have to say about the murder?"

I blow on the tea, cupping it in both hands and letting the steam waft up toward my face. "He said the killer we're looking for is way too close."

"Clearly. He knows we're on the case. Which means he knows O'Neil talked to us."

"He's as good as dead if there is someone inside that prison on this guy's payroll." I blow on the tea one more time before finally taking a sip.

"I can't believe this guy stuck around after getting away with murder."

"Maybe he stuck around to make sure he did. Keeping an eye on O'Neil and such," I say, lowering the tea to my lap, which is currently covered with a throw blanket. "Hey, what happened to the Playboy bunny mugs you used to have?" He told me they were a gag gift from his brother.

"I got rid of them. Nick will never know. It's not like we ever see each other, and to be honest, I don't think he really intended for me to keep the mugs. They were just a joke." Mitchell's family life is more than a little depressing.

"I like these better," I say, holding up the plain black mug. "They're simple yet elegant."

Mitchell laughs. "It's okay, Piper. You don't always have to try to make me feel better when my family comes up. And that mug cost one dollar. There's nothing elegant about it."

"I love a good deal," I say with a smile.

He leans his head back on the couch and looks at me, but he doesn't say anything.

"You look tired," I say. "You don't have to sit up with me while I drink this."

"I'm not sure how much sleep I'm going to be able to

get considering this killer just took out our only lead mere feet from us."

I know exactly what he means. "Which begs the question, why didn't he come inside the house and shoot us, too?"

"I guess he didn't want to out himself to us."

No. I shake my head. "Try again."

"He didn't want to kill more people than he had to?"

No. "I don't think he has a problem with killing. How about I take a stab at this?" I say.

Mitchell turns up his palm, indicating I have the floor.

"I think he wasn't certain he'd be able to take out both of us before you shot him."

Mitchell smiles and shakes his head. "You think I'm the reason our lives weren't threatened? You give me too much credit."

"Really? Because you had your gun drawn before I could turn around. You just reacted. And you made sure I was safe."

"That's my job."

I'm not sure if he means keeping specifically *me* safe or just people in general. I finish the rest of my tea in two big gulps.

"Wow, someone is trying to get rid of me," he says.

"It's your house. If I wanted to get rid of you, I'd go home."

"Except you can't. Your father would kill me if I let you leave, especially after Hugo was murdered tonight."

He rubs his forehead. "Is it just me, or do these cases keep getting worse?"

I let out a deep breath. "That's tough to say. We've worked some pretty awful cases. Need I remind you of the times I was drugged through visions or the underground *Phantom of the Opera* hostage situation?"

Mitchell lowers his hand and stares at me. "I wonder if other towns have problems like these. Maybe it's us. Maybe we attract these lunatics."

"I'm pretty sure crazy people exist everywhere in the world. We're just good at catching them."

He places his hand on my knee and gives it a gentle squeeze. "We make a good team." He stands up. "Good night, partner."

"Good night," I say, watching him walk out of the living room. I reach for the lamp beside the couch and turn it off. Then I snuggle under the throw blanket. It smells like Mitchell, and I'm not sure if I'm comforted by the fact that I like that or if it scares the hell out of me.

I wake up and have to look around to figure out where I am. This isn't my room or my bed. And on the dresser is the framed photograph of me sitting on Mitchell's lap when he played Santa at the ski lodge on Christmas. "Damn him," I say as I toss the covers off me. I open the bedroom door and storm out to the living room, where Mitchell is already up and drinking coffee.

"Morning, sunshine. Sleep well?" he asks with a smile.

"You picked me up and carried me into your bed?" I throw my arm behind me, gesturing toward his room for emphasis.

"A gentleman does not allow a woman to sleep on the couch when there is a perfectly comfortable bed available. Besides, once I figured out why you didn't want to sleep in my bed, I knew there wasn't going to be an issue. I told you it's a new bed with clean sheets. You weren't going to read anything off that thing except for maybe me snoring."

"You do snore. You woke up Jez last time you slept on my couch," I say, crossing my arms. I expect him to fight back and tell me I snore too, but instead he says something that shuts me right up.

"FYI, you're the only woman who has ever stayed the night here."

Jeffrey whistles in his cage.

I can't deal with whatever this is between us this early in the morning, so I point to his coffee mug. "Is there more in the kitchen?"

He starts to get up but thinks better of it and says, "Help yourself."

I whirl around and head to the kitchen. It's small, mostly because there's a big island in the center with seating. I go right to the coffeepot and reach for the cabinet above it. My hand wraps around the knob.

"I should bring her coffee. She's going to be so angry with me for moving her while she slept, but I couldn't let her sleep on the couch. That thing is so uncomfortable. But if I bring her coffee in bed, she's going to read too much into it. She reads into everything I do now. I never should have told her the truth. She can't handle it. It was stupid and selfish of me. But she's my partner and best friend. I couldn't exactly lie to her either."

"Piper?" Mitchell physically removes my hand from the cabinet. "What did you see?"

"Nothing. Just that the coffee mugs are in here."

He continues to eye me as he opens the cabinet and pulls out a mug. "You're a terrible liar."

"So are you."

"Uh-oh. How bad was it? The vision?" He pours the coffee and hands me the mug before leaning back on the counter and crossing his arms in front of him. He's guarding himself from what I'm about to say.

"I really didn't see much. It was more of what I heard." I look down at the coffee and take a deep breath. "Oh my God." I bring the mug to my nose and inhale deeply. "You bought toasted almond coffee."

"I didn't even realize that's what I'd made," he says, suddenly looking panicked.

I can't believe I didn't smell it sooner, but I'm so used to smelling it that it didn't register. "I'm never here. Why would you buy this? You don't even order it from Marcia's."

"She's the one who gave it to me. She didn't even let me pay for it." He shoves his hands in his pockets. "She asked me if I'd give it to you. But that was when we had that fight. I wound up bringing it here, and I sort of forgot about it. When I opened the bag to make coffee this morning, it didn't even dawn on me what it was."

"Oh." That makes sense.

"You can take the rest of the bag. I mean, it was meant for you."

"It's okay. I might be staying here for a few more days anyway until the case is closed. Keep it here."

"You sure?" he asks, looking relieved.

"Yeah. Can we swing by my place so I can shower and get clean clothes?" Mitchell is already showered and ready to go.

"Sure. I have disposable coffee cups. I'll transfer yours into one so you can take it with us."

I smirk at him. "Silly man." I raise the mug to my lips and tip the contents back. "Ah," I say, once I've chugged the entire mug. "I'll take my refill in the disposable cup."

He laughs and does just that as I bring the mug to the sink and wash it.

"I do have bad news for you," he says after I return the dish towel to the bar on the stove.

"We have to go to the station to talk to Chief Johansen, don't we?"

"One cup of coffee and you're already on top of your game." He flashes me a smile.

An hour later, I'm showered, have on clean clothes, and am wiping my face after Jez bathed me in kisses. Dad brought her to my office so I could see her. "Why did I never think to bring her to work with me before?" I ask. "She's so well behaved, and she definitely perks up the place."

"Probably because we're never here much. We're always out investigating. You've been stalling long enough, Piper. We have to go see Chief Johansen."

"What does he want?" Dad asks, and I can tell he doesn't have a lot of love left for his former chief.

"Updates. And he won't be happy," Mitchell says.

"I don't see why I have to go," I whine. "I don't work there."

"You're a consultant on this case. You have to go with me."

I'm fighting really hard not to stamp my foot and cry, "But I don't wanna." Jez puts her head on my leg. "Maybe we should bring Jezebel. She could distract him for us."

"Johansen isn't scary in the least, pumpkin. Once you let him know you can handle your own cases without interference, he'll back right off."

Except this is the first time he's interfered. All thanks to Officer Andrews. "I just need to know what it was Hugo knew."

"Are you saying you want to read Hugo?" Mitchell asks me.

"Want to? No, not at all. Need to? Most likely."

"Want me to go along?" Dad asks. "I can bring Jez to my house and then meet you both at the station."

"Actually, I need you to do me a different favor. I need you to interview Hugo's wife. Find out if he ever talked about O'Neil at home. It's possible whatever he knew, she heard about at home."

"You got it."

"Thanks, Dad."

Mitchell and I head to the station since I can't stall any longer. I try to pretend I don't notice the smile on Officer Andrews's face as we walk past his desk. But when he says, "Brennan, heard you failed to stop a murder from four feet away," I can't help myself.

I stop, turn on my heel, and walk right over to his desk. "Andrews, does your wife know you have another woman's underwear in the glove compartment of your car?"

The entire station goes silent. Chief Johansen steps out of his office, hands on hips, and his eyes volley between Officer Andrews and me. "Brennan, Ashwell, my office," he barks before disappearing inside.

Officer Andrews is just glaring at me. Mitchell has to physically push me toward the chief's office.

"I was channeling his anger," I whisper to Mitchell. "I didn't mean to say that. I don't even know that it's true."

"Oh, it's true all right. Did you see his face? It was like he was trying to figure out when you managed to read him without him knowing."

This is not how I planned to use my abilities. I don't want to stoop to Officer Andrews's level.

Mitchell knocks on Chief Johansen's open door to announce our arrival.

"Shut the door behind you," the chief says, without looking up from the file on his desk.

I step inside but don't sit down.

"Have a seat," Chief Johansen says.

"No, thank you. I'll stand." I have to distance myself from all the anger flying around this station this morning, or I'm going to completely lose my mind.

Mitchell stands with me, but I can tell doing so is making him uncomfortable. I don't want to get him in trouble with his boss, so I dip my head in the direction of the chair. He doesn't move, though.

"Care to tell me why I have a dead prison guard on my hands when you were with him at the time he was killed?" Chief Johansen asks.

"Ms. Ashwell and I were in the victim's living room. He left to answer a knock on the door, which he told us was most likely the security guard in the community following up on our visit."

"There was no reason to think we'd been followed," I say. "Or that anyone else was at the door."

"No reason?" Chief Johansen's brow furrows, and he puts down the pen that was previously in his right hand. "You went to the prison to interrogate an inmate whom you suspect might be in danger. But you didn't think to report that you were following up on a lead with a guard who left under suspicious circumstances after your arrival at the prison? And you didn't think that the killer O'Neil is protecting might also try to eliminate anyone who might be looking to prove his guilt?" He laces his fingers in front of him on the desk. "Should I keep going?"

"It's my fault you weren't notified," I say. "Mitchell—Detective Brennan was about to call you when I stopped him. I wasn't sure about the lead I was following and didn't want to alert you until I knew it wasn't a false alarm."

"You have no authority over *Detective Brennan's* actions." He stresses "Detective Brennan," letting me know he not only noticed my slipup in calling Mitchell by his first name, but he didn't care for it one bit.

"I accept full responsibility," Mitchell says. "I should have called it in."

I study Chief Johansen's face and realize he's going to nail Mitchell on this. Johansen never met me before because he didn't want to. He doesn't like that Mitchell brings me on these cases, and he used me to try to get Mitchell to screw up. I move toward Chief Johansen's desk and grab his pen before he can even try to stop me.

"That damn woman has put this station through enough. It was one thing when Thomas was still here. He had this entire town's respect, so people were willing to overlook the use of a psychic on police investigations. But now, she's making us look bad. She humiliated Andrews,

and I've been dealing with phone calls ever since. It has to stop."

"I said, hand me my pen," Chief Johansen bellows. He's on his feet with his hand outstretched, palm up.

Mitchell removes the pen from my hand and places it on Chief Johansen's palm.

"Ms. Ashwell, consider yourself removed from this case and any future cases with the Weltunkin PD. Your services are no longer wanted."

CHAPTER TEN

Mitchell's entire body goes rigid. He's about to explode.

I place my hand on his arm. "It's fine," I tell him.

He shakes his head. "No, it's not. I wouldn't have solved half of these cases without you. You're more valuable to this station than all the other officers combined." Mitchell turns to the chief. "You can't fire her. She's our best shot at finding this guy. You've never seen her in action, Chief. She's amazing. She's saved so many people."

"He thinks I'm giving the station a bad reputation," I say. "He thinks I made Officer Andrews look bad." I want him to know what I saw in my vision. Not only to prove what I can do, but so he can hear how ludicrous it actually sounds. "I'm sorry if people have been calling about the last cold case, but that wasn't a case I failed on. Officer Andrews neglected to solve that kidnapping, which was actually a murder. I wasn't even working with the WPD at the time. But I offered to work with Officer Andrews so he could clear his own name and reputation. He chose not to take me up on that offer."

Chief Johansen spins a file on his desk to face me, and I see it's not O'Neil's file at all. It's Mitchell's. "Detective Brennan, I've gotten several complaints since you started working with Ms. Ashwell. You've broken protocol for her on numerous occasions. You've looked the other way when she's neglected to follow procedure. I've been more than forgiving, but seeing as how I'm a generous man, I'm going to give you two options. You can turn in your badge and serve a suspension, during which time you will review proper protocol, or you can permanently cease working with Ms. Ashwell and be assigned to a partner here at the station."

There is no choice. He's already fired me. "He'll take the partner," I say.

"Piper." Mitchell grabs my arm.

I stare him straight in the eye. "Take the partner," I say. "Trust me on this."

He lets go of me.

"How long has this been going on?" Chief Johansen asks, motioning between us.

"We've been working together since before her father retired," Mitchell says.

"That's not what I mean, and you know it."

Realization dawns on me. "We're not dating. We're

partners. Mitchell saved my life, so yeah, I call him Mitchell and not Detective Brennan. He's worked beside me and put his own life on the line for me. That's what partners do. And you think he's broken protocol by following my leads, but what am I here for if not to give the department leads? I solve cases for you. Maybe not in the way another police detective would, but I get results. I've saved people. And yeah, Officer Andrews hates me, but did you ever consider that the reason he hates me so much is because I've forced him to realize the flaws in himself? I'm not perfect, Chief. I'm going to make mistakes just like everyone else. But know that taking me off a case isn't going to make me stop having visions, and I won't sit on those visions and do nothing. I'm a licensed private investigator, and I will track down this killer with or without the help of the WPD."

I nod to Mitchell before turning on my heel and walking out of the office. Officer Andrews is standing right outside the door, and I don't doubt he heard every word that was said in there. I stare at him. "You chose this war between us. I tried to help you multiple times. You wanted this, and you got exactly what you asked for."

"I did. You got canned." He smirks. "I couldn't be happier."

"Since I'm no longer working with the WPD, I have no reservations about telling your wife everything I know."

He grabs my arm, but Officer Wallace marches over to us. "Take your hand off her, Andrews."

I yank my arm from his grasp and smile at Officer Wallace. "Tell Harry I'm going to miss working with him," I say before walking out of the station.

Mom pours me another glass of unsweetened iced tea. "I never liked the chief," she says. "Your father didn't have trouble with him, but just about everyone else at the station has."

"It doesn't seem like Officer Andrews does," I say, scratching the top of Jezebel's head, which is in my lap.

"He has in the past. Officer Andrews isn't well liked, and Chief Johansen has reprimanded him more than once about how he conducts himself around the other officers.

"Then why is he listening to him now?" I know Officer Andrews is behind all of this. I can feel it like a brick in my stomach. A brick I'd like to smash right over Andrews's head.

"Piper, you've always faced people who dislike you solely for what you can do. They don't understand it, and that scares them."

"So, Officer Andrews is afraid of me, and, therefore, he found a way to get rid of me?"

"Worse. He made the chief of police fear you." She's right. He put enough doubt in the chief's head for him to give me this impossible case. He set me up to fail so he'd have grounds to dismiss me.

Something else comes to me as an absolute truth. "Chief Johansen is afraid of Dad. That's why he didn't try something like this sooner. He knew everyone in town loved Dad when he was on the force, and they wouldn't support the chief firing me on account that I'm Dad's daughter. But now that Dad's been retired for a while and people don't see him in uniform all the time, the chief thinks it's safe to get rid of me without getting backlash from the community."

The front door opens, and Dad comes storming right into the kitchen. "I just got off the phone with Mitchell."

"Tell me he didn't do something stupid and get himself fired." It would be just like him to do so.

"No. But he told me all about your conversation with Johansen. I knew I should have gone to the station with you. I just knew it." He slaps his hand against the side of his leg, and Jez rushes to his side. I'm not sure if she's sensing his anger or if she thinks he was giving a command with his hand gesture. Dad bends down and kisses the top of her head.

"What happens now?" Mom asks.

"I have a case to solve," I say. "I don't need the WPD to employ me."

"Piper, the only way you can look into this is if O'Neil hires you." His mouth curves into a smirk. "Or if someone can get Mrs. Spencer to hire the Ashwell Agency to solve her husband's murder."

I smile at Dad. "You got Hugo's wife to hire us."

He shrugs. "If Johansen wants a fight, he's got himself one. He'll be sorry he fired you when we make the entire station look bad by solving this case for them."

"What about Mitchell?" I ask.

Mom gives me a knowing look. "What about him, Piper?"

"I don't want him to get fired because of me," I say, not about to reveal that Chief Johansen thought we were dating. Mom would start thinking up baby names for all her grandchildren, and then I'd have to break her heart by telling her kids are not in my future.

"Mitchell said he's been temporarily assigned to a new partner." Dad lowers his gaze.

Oh no. "Don't say it. Please don't say it, Dad."

"I'm sorry, pumpkin, but Chief Johansen felt the only way to be sure Mitchell didn't work with you on this case was if his new partner is Andrews."

It's a nightmare. I place my head in my hands, elbows on the kitchen table. "That means I have to solve this case without Mitchell."

"I think you mean *we* have to," Dad says. "And it wasn't so long ago you were begging me not to become Mitchell's partner."

"A lot has changed since then." I went from hating the man, to mildly disliking him, to tolerating him, to being his friend, to...I don't know what.

"There is another solution," Mom says, and I detect a

hint of a smile in her voice, so I raise my head to look at her.

"What are you scheming?" I ask.

"Well, the chief can stop you two from working together, but he has no jurisdiction when it comes to Mitchell's personal life."

"I'm not following."

Dad starts laughing. "Bonnie, I do think you're going to give Piper her first gray hair."

"What am I missing here, you two?" I look back and forth between them.

Mom places her hand on top of mine. "You tell me, Ms. Psychic P.I."

I stare at her, trying to figure out what crazy plan she's concocted in that pretty head of hers. And then it hits me. "No. That's crazy."

"Is it, though?" Mom asks before taking a sip of her iced tea.

The doorbell rings, and Dad motions that he'll get it.

"Mom, I fail to see what purpose pretending to date Mitchell will serve in this case."

"Actually, that's not a bad plan," Mitchell says.

I look up to see him standing beside Dad.

"How are you here? Dad said Andrews is your new partner."

"Lunch break. I ditched him."

I get up and look out the small window above the kitchen sink. "And you don't think he'd stoop so low as to follow you?" Across the street, I spot the patrol car. "He's out there right now," I say, whirling around on Mitchell.

"Well then, I guess the solution is obvious," Mom says, getting up to bring her glass to the sink. "If you two were dating, it would be perfectly normal for Mitchell to stop by to see you on his lunch break." She's enjoying this far too much.

"You know, pumpkin, I have to agree with your mother."

"Great. Thanks, Dad."

Mitchell gently takes me by my elbow. "Can I talk to you outside?"

I roll my eyes, but I allow him to lead me to the front porch. We sit down, and I wave to Officer Andrews. I'm really tempted to give him the middle finger, but Mitchell suspects as much and takes my hand in his to stop me. "I hate that man so much."

"You're in good company there." Mitchell turns my face so I'm looking at him. "Piper, I know you hate this idea, but it could be the solution we're looking for. If we go along with this, we'd have a reason to be together that has nothing to do with the case. Of course, we'll be discussing the case and working on leads, but only we'll know that. Then when we solve the case together, we can come clean, and Chief Johansen will have to see the value you bring to the WPD."

"I see your point, but I'm not sure I could pull it off. I

mean, I'm awful with physical contact, and who is going to believe we're dating when I can't even—"

"Hold my hand?" He raises my hand, which is still in his, between us. "It's like I told you. When you don't realize you're letting your wall down, you can control your visions." He tilts his head in the direction of the patrol car. "And right now, I'm pretty sure we're convincing Andrews that we're more than just partners on these cases."

I still haven't removed my hand from his, and even though it's my right hand, I haven't read him either. "What if I can't keep this up? I mean, right now, it's just you and me here. But if we have to do this in front of other people, I could easily freak out and start reading you."

"We're in front of three people right now."

"Three?" I turn to the kitchen window and see Mom's and Dad's faces practically pressed up against the glass. I laugh. "They're impossible. I swear. Sometimes I feel like I'm the parent and they're two rebellious teenagers."

"Well, in this situation, you're more like the rebellious teenager. We are concocting a plan to trick the entire police department, after all."

"Point taken." I look out at Officer Andrews again. "I really do want to go to his wife and tell her everything. I don't know her at all, but she has to deserve better than him."

He brushes my hair behind my shoulder. "You can't save everyone. She knows he's cheated. You've seen that. What she chooses to do with that knowledge is up to her."

"You're right, but I think you can stop touching my hair and holding my hand now. Officer Andrews is pulling away."

Mitchell lets go of my hand and places his palms flat on his thighs. "Right. Sorry."

"Dad got Mrs. Spencer to hire the Ashwell Agency to find out who murdered her husband. So, I'm thinking he and I need to get to the morgue so I can read one of his personal effects."

"Good thinking. I have to get back to the station anyway. Lunch is over, which is why Andrews left." Mitchell stands up. "Hey, are you staying at my condo again tonight?"

"Yes, she is," Mom says through the kitchen window.

"Good Lord, this couldn't be more embarrassing."

Mitchell laughs. "Hey, it plays into the whole dating thing."

"Does it?" I ask. "I mean, I doubt anyone at the station has any trouble believing you'd engage in premarital sex, but I'm a completely different story."

"I promise not to smear your good name too much," he jokes. "Besides, we know the truth."

The problem is he's right. We both do know the truth: I have real feelings for Mitchell.

"I'll check in with you later to see what you found out from Mrs. Spencer and to let you know what Andrews and I uncover." He rolls his eyes at the mention of his new partner.

I nod and watch him get into his patrol car.

Dad comes out onto the porch as Mitchell's taillights disappear down the street. "So..."

"Don't even say it." I hold up my hand for emphasis.

"Say what?" Dad smirks and pulls his car keys from his pants pocket. "I was merely going to say it's time to head to Mrs. Spencer's house."

"Sure you were." I get in the passenger seat of Dad's BMW.

Mom waves from the front door, a huge smile on her face.

"She does know this is fake, right? Mitchell and I are only pretending."

Dad gives me a look as he pulls out of the driveway. "Pumpkin, you are far too perceptive to believe that."

"Mitchell and I are not really dating."

"Call it what you want, or don't label it at all. It doesn't change the truth."

"I am not having this conversation with you." I cross my arms in my seat.

"So you keep saying, yet here we are."

I refuse to talk for the rest of the drive to Mrs. Spencer's house. She greets us with puffy, red eyes and a tissue in hand.

"Please come in," she says in a shaky voice. Her eyes are trained on me. "You were here when it happened, weren't you?"

"Yes."

"How is it that there were two witnesses yet no one saw anything?" she asks, motioning for us to go into the living room.

I walk over to the photograph on the mantel. "I was looking at this when it happened," I tell her.

"That was taken on our anniversary last year." She walks up alongside me. "Do you have any idea who did this?"

"That's a difficult question to answer. I know this person has killed someone before, but I don't know his identity."

"But you will find him. Your father said you're psychic."

"I am, and I'll do my best to find the person responsible for Hugo's death."

She reaches into her pocket and pulls out a watch. "This was Hugo's. I bought it for him." She places it in my hand, eager to have me get right to work. It's nice not to have to explain myself, but she wants answers right this very second, which puts a whole lot of pressure on me.

Dad gives me a small nod. "Mrs. Spencer, why don't we sit down and give Piper a little space? She works better that way."

"Yes, of course." She follows him to the couch.

I take one more look at the image of Hugo in the photograph before wrapping my fingers around the watch and closing my eyes.

"She's here," Hugo says into his phone.

"Very good. Now keep an eye on her, and tell me what she finds out."

"No. That wasn't the deal. I'm getting out of here. She's psychic. If she sees me, she'll figure out I'm spying on her." He glances at the watch on his wrist. "I have to go now."

"Do not cross me, Spencer."

Hugo hangs up.

I open my eyes and look at Dad. "Hugo knew who the killer was. He was communicating with him."

CHAPTER ELEVEN

"What?" Mrs. Spencer's voice is shrill. She's on the verge of totally cracking. "What are you saying?"

Dad stands up and walks over to me. "Did you see him?"

"No. Hugo was on the phone with him. He called him to tell him I was at the prison. He was supposed to spy on me for the killer, but he refused. He hung up the phone and left the prison."

"He disobeyed the killer," Dad says.

"And it got him killed." Hugo was both trying to protect O'Neil and working for the killer. It's completely crazy. He got himself smack in the middle of the two men.

"I know what you're thinking," Dad says.

Mrs. Spencer jumps to her feet. "Well, I don't. Someone needs to explain this to me. Now."

"Mrs. Spencer, I think your husband was trying to

help Mr. O'Neil because he believed he was innocent. But he wound up getting caught between him and the real killer. The killer was forcing your husband to spy on O'Neil and me."

"You're the reason he was shot," she says in a small voice.

What? No! How can she say that?

She holds out her hand. "Give me my husband's watch, and get out of my house."

She can't be serious. I stare at her with wide eyes and hand her the watch, which she practically rips from my hand.

"Mrs. Spencer, I understand you're grieving, but Piper is not the reason your husband is dead."

"He refused to do what the killer wanted," I say. "That's why he was killed."

"My husband tried to protect you, and look where that got him. Look where that got me! I'm a widow because of you!" She's screaming now.

"Piper, let's go," Dad says, tugging on my arm.

"Mrs. Spencer, I'm very sorry about your husband, and I plan to find the man who did this to him." I can't be angry with her. I know she's lashing out at me because she can't turn her anger on the real guilty party.

She turns her back to me and sobs uncontrollably. I hate to leave her alone like this, but my presence is only upsetting her more. I walk to the door. Dad hangs back for a moment to talk to her. If anyone can offer her any comfort right now, it's him. I get in the car and wait, leaning my head against the seat and rubbing my forehead.

My phone chimes with a text, so I grab it from my pocket.

Mitchell: My new partner has managed to insult me six times in the past four minutes. How are you doing?

Piper: Six times? That's nothing. My record is much higher.

Mitchell: LOL True but at least I know you mean your insults in a nice way.

Piper: Right. Well, that's the definition of insult, isn't it?

Mitchell: I miss you.

I don't know how to respond to that, so I pocket my phone instead.

Dad gets in the car. "You okay?"

"Yeah, I just feel awful I caused her that much pain."

Dad places his hand on mine. "You didn't, pumpkin. The killer did. And when we catch him, Mrs. Spencer will assign blame to the real guilty party. You'll see."

"Where to now?" I ask him, at a loss for where to go from here.

"I'm thinking the morgue." He backs out of the driveway. "Unless you're not up for it."

"I'm fine. I just want to catch this guy before something happens to O'Neil." A thought slams into me.

"Wait! I need to talk to the security guard stationed at the gate."

"Of this community?" Dad asks.

"Yes."

Dad nods. "Because he must have let this guy in."

"Or the killer knew the keypad access code to get in on his own," I say.

Dad turns to look at me. "Fact?"

I nod.

"So he might live here," Dad says.

"Drive around. Maybe I'll sense him."

"How, Piper? You only heard his voice in your vision, right? That's not enough for you to go on."

I have nothing else. I have to try this. "If I can't sense him, we'll head to the morgue, but we can't leave without trying this first."

Dad nods. He slows the car, driving at basically a crawl past the houses. I lower my window and reach out with my right hand, as if that will allow me to feel this guy's energy from inside the car. I know I'm being crazy, but I can't seem to stop myself either.

"When did he tell you?" Dad asks.

"Who tell me what?" I wiggle my fingers in the air.

"Mitchell. He told you about our conversation."

"Dad, I told you I don't want to talk about it."

"Okay, then can we talk about your grandmother?"

Grandma Maywood eventually pushed her entire family, including my grandfather and my mother, away because Mom witnessed her having a vision and got really scared by it. "If you're going to tell me to learn from her experience and not let my abilities stand in the way of having a normal life, you can save your breath."

"Actually, I was going to say you have something she didn't."

"And what's that?"

"A support system. You've never had to hide what you do from me, your mother, or Mitchell. We all know. And Mitchell can calm you down after a vision like no one else can."

"I get it, Dad. He's good for me. But I also can't forget the kind of person he was before he met me." I do believe he's changed, but my memory of the way he was before becoming my partner is still crystal clear.

"Believe me, I'm not going to forget it either."

Except he doesn't really know. He didn't see what I saw in visions. He doesn't even know Mitchell's mother was psychic.

"Whoa!" I wiggle my fingers again. "Stop the car."

Dad immediately applies the brakes. "What did you feel?"

"I'm not sure, but my senses are tingling." I stare at the brick house. It's not one of the largest homes in the development, but it's pristine. The lawn is perfectly manicured. The bushes are expertly trimmed.

"Can you sense if anyone is home?" Dad asks, ducking his head to better see the house out my window.

"No, I can't." Walking up to the front door and having the killer answer is suicide. He knows who I am. He'd shoot me on the spot. "Wait. It's not a male I'm sensing. It's a female."

"A female? Who?"

I open my door and step out of the car.

"Piper, wait." Dad hurries out of the car to join me. "Neither of us is armed. We should call Mitchell."

"No, he'll have to bring Officer Andrews, and I don't trust him not to botch this up."

"If the killer is here, we're both as good as dead if we go any closer to the house."

I take a deep breath. "Mrs. Spencer wasn't completely wrong. Hugo put his life on the line for me. I owe him this much."

Dad grabs my arm. "You know Mitchell wouldn't let you go up to that front door."

"Are you kidding me? Mitchell would be storming the house right beside me."

"I'm calling him," Dad says, his phone already in hand.

"Fine." I walk to the mailbox, hoping it will have a last name on it, but it doesn't. A green sign on the front lawn reads 245. I check the street sign. Booker Drive. Committing the address to my memory, I move to the side of the house. The backyard is fenced in, so I can't see anything. I move closer, and Dad comes with me, finished with his call.

The fence is about six feet tall. "Give me a boost. I need to see what's back there," I tell Dad.

"We don't have a warrant. Right now, we are trespassing."

"Stirrup hands." I demonstrate by lacing my fingers together.

"We are waiting for Mitchell," Dad asserts.

I huff and look around the yard for something to give me a boost. There's a bucket by the hose on the side of the house, so I walk over, grab it, and place it upside down on the ground in front of the fence. I step up onto it and peer over the fence. The backyard, while mowed, isn't as well maintained as the front yard. And one place in particular is greener than the rest of the grass. The grass is also slightly longer there.

I turn back to Dad. "They replanted the grass in one spot, and I think I know why."

"Recently replanted?

No. "Not recently, but it's newer than the rest."

"How new?" Dad asks.

Five years. "He buried Amelia Crane in the backyard," I say.

Dad has his phone to his ear again. "We have probable cause to search the property," he says, and I know he's talking to Mitchell. The problem is Mitchell isn't alone, and his new partner won't see my psychic abilities as evidence to give us probable cause. He's going to stop Mitchell from forcing entry into this gated community.

I have an idea, though. One that will hopefully piss off Officer Andrews enough that he'll break a few rules. "We need Harry," I tell Dad. "Call Officer Wallace."

"I'm calling for Wallace and Harry now," Dad says into the phone.

"Tell Mitchell I said they aren't needed."

Dad picks up on what I'm doing and smirks as he says, "Piper said you and Officer Andrews aren't needed."

I can hear yelling on the other end, and even though I can't make out what's being said, I know it's Officer Andrews who is doing all the screaming. I'm sure he's slinging choice words at me.

Dad hangs up and calls Officer Wallace. "Wallace, it's Ashwell. We need you and Harry at 245 Booker Drive as soon as possible. We have a possible dead body buried in the backyard."

I know Officer Wallace won't question me, so I direct my attention to the house. I haven't heard any sounds come from inside, and if anyone is home, they'd definitely hear Dad and me. I'm almost positive the house is empty.

Besides, this guy isn't stupid. After he killed Hugo Spencer right here in this community, he probably left. He wouldn't stick around where he could possibly get caught. And that means he won't leave O'Neil alive for much longer either.

"We need to make sure someone at the prison is looking out for O'Neil," I tell Dad as I step off the bucket. "He's in more danger now than ever."

Dad takes a deep breath. "That means we're in danger, too. O'Neil is a loose end, and we know about him. If this guy killed Spencer because Spencer wouldn't spy on you, then he knows you know O'Neil is innocent. You're no safer. Actually, you're in more danger since you don't have a prison full of guards protecting you."

I can't think about that right now. All I care about is digging up Amelia Crane's body and finally putting her case to rest. She deserves that much.

Despite Dad telling Mitchell we don't need him and Officer Andrews, Mitchell's patrol car pulls up out front, and Officer Andrews comes storming over to us, gun in hand.

"We haven't knocked on the door," I tell Mitchell, intent on ignoring Officer Andrews as much as possible.

Mitchell steps up on the bucket I was using. "Good eye, Piper. The grass is definitely being fertilized more in that one spot."

That's an awful way to put it, but he's right.

"I'm knocking on the door," Officer Andrews says.

Mitchell, Dad, and I follow him. He knocks on the door and yells, "WPD, open up!"

I roll my eyes because I'm pretty sure no killer in history ever willingly opened their door after an announcement like that.

As I predicted, no one comes to the door. I move back around to the side of the house at the same time Officer Wallace arrives with Harry. I don't dare greet Harry because he's working and fully in the zone. I point to the gate, not wanting to break Harry's concentration.

Mitchell tries the lock on the gate, but it doesn't budge. The one day I don't carry my purse, which always contains a lock pick kit. He looks at Officer Andrews. "Do we agree we have probable cause?"

Dad's on his phone. "This house belongs to Wilson McDonald."

I'm not surprised he was busy researching. Dad has to always be doing something to keep a case moving forward.

Officer Andrews calls the station and asks for a background check on McDonald. Is he seriously going to stop us from checking this backyard?

I need something concrete. Some evidence that there's a body buried in that yard. I look at Harry. "Officer Wallace, can Harry sniff out a dead body from this far away?"

"No, sorry, Piper, but he'd need to be closer."

I don't have anything that belonged to Amelia, so there isn't even any scent of hers to sniff out. I'm stuck. All thanks to Officer Andrews. I never should have let Dad call Mitchell. It was a huge mistake.

Mitchell meets my gaze and stands beside me. "Can you sense Amelia?"

"No. But you saw the ground. It makes sense. I'm not even going off of my abilities here, yet Officer Andrews is going to dismiss anything I say."

Mitchell turns and glares at his partner, who is still on

the phone. I squint at Officer Andrews and realize who he's talking to at the station.

"Bastard," I mumble, walking over and yanking the phone from his hand. "Chief Johansen," I say, moving away from Officer Andrews. Mitchell intercedes by blocking Andrews's path to me.

"Ashwell, you are off this case. What the hell are you doing there?" Chief Johansen yells into the phone.

"I was hired by Mrs. Spencer to find her husband's killer. I have every right to be here."

"You can't search that property. You're trespassing."

"Detective Brennan shares my opinion about the grass in the backyard. If you let this body continue to rot there and I uncover it, you will be making the WPD look stupid. That will be on you. I'm just giving you a friendly warning." Without another word, I hand the phone back to Officer Andrews. "Your ego is what's making you look bad. Your success rate would be so much better if you'd listen to me for once."

Officer Andrews puts the phone to his ear and walks away from me.

"Piper, making him angry isn't helping," Dad says.

"Screw this," Mitchell says. "I'm the lead detective on this case. Wallace, get Harry in there."

"What about the chief?" I ask him.

"He didn't tell me no because I never talked to him. Andrews did." He winks at me.

"Want me to cut off that lock?" Officer Wallace asks Mitchell.

Mitchell nods. "And do it quickly." He's glaring at the back of Officer Andrews's head.

While Officer Wallace gets to work, Mitchell leans toward me, pressing his arm against mine. "If I get fired, I can come work with you and your dad, right?"

"I'm not letting you get fired," I say. "We're going to find Amelia's body, and both Chief Johansen and Officer Andrews won't have a thing to say."

Officer Andrews storms over to us once the lock on the gate is cut off, but Harry immediately starts sniffing the ground. He goes directly to the patch of grass that drew my attention and barks.

I meet Officer Andrews's gaze. "You're welcome," I say. "Maybe one of these days, we can skip the song and dance to get to this point."

"That day might come sooner than you think. Chief Johansen wants to see you in his office right now."

"I don't answer to Chief Johansen, so I'm going to have to decline that invitation. Feel free to relay the message." I cross my arms, turn on my heel, and meet up with Mitchell, Dad, and Officer Wallace as they dig up the ground. Harry is patiently sitting beside the hole, watching.

Mitchell notices me and takes a break to talk. He wipes sweat from his brow before saying, "What did Andrews say to you?"

"Just that the chief wants to talk to me. I told him I'm not going to the station."

Mitchell looks over my shoulder at Officer Andrews. "He's on the phone again. You know he's going to try to pin something on you. Some bogus charge to force you back to the station."

"Like trespassing?" I ask, looking up at the house. For the first time, I get an eerie feeling coming from inside.

"What is it?" Mitchell asks.

The curtain is closed, so I can't see in through the sliding glass door on the back deck, but my senses have no trouble getting past them. "Is it still considered trespassing when the homeowner isn't alive?"

"What?" Mitchell's eyes widen.

"Wilson McDonald is dead. His body is inside the house."

CHAPTER TWELVE

I move toward the back deck, but I don't get far before Officer Andrews says, "Whoa. I don't think so, Ashwell. You are not going inside that house. I've overlooked a lot, but I'm not letting this slide."

Overlooked what exactly? He watches me like a hawk and calls me out on everything. "I don't think this place is even locked up," I say, more to Mitchell than Officer Andrews.

"There's a dead body in there. I can feel it." It says a lot that feeling dead bodies is a thing now. That's not exactly a sense I'd been hoping to expand upon, yet here I am. I sniffed out two dead bodies better than Harry did.

"Do you seriously let her get away with this? All because you're dating her?" Officer Andrews asks, and that's about the last straw I can take.

"Unlike you, Mitchell is not an idiot. He doesn't

dismiss a lead, especially one this huge. And whether or not Mitchell and I are dating is no concern of yours. You should spend a little more time worrying about your failing marriage. Keep your pointy nose out of my personal life."

He steps toward me, but Mitchell places his hand on his chest to stop him. Officer Andrews quickly swats it away. "You never showed me the same curtesy, Ashwell. I don't owe you anything."

"Don't—"

I hold up my hand to stop Mitchell. "He's right. This one's on me." I inhale deeply. "You're right, Officer. I was out of line when I read you against your will. I understand why you've never forgiven me for that despite the times I've helped you out. And I'm sorry. I invaded your privacy, and I shouldn't have. You have my apologies for *that*." I stress the last word. "But I will not apologize for following the leads my abilities give me. This is how I work. It's how I save people. If you have a problem with that, then it's something you're going to have to learn to deal with because that's on you."

"Seriously, how can you hold such a grudge after all she's done for you," Mitchell asks him.

Officer Andrews narrows his eyes at me. "You told him, didn't you? The one time I actually came to you for help, and you couldn't keep your mouth shut. You ran off to tell your boyfriend."

I know Mitchell was trying to help, but he just made

things so much worse. "You know what, it doesn't matter. Nothing I do matters because you're always going to hate me. You hate what I can do because it makes me a better detective than you'll ever be." I whip my arm out in the direction of the sliding glass door. "I know there's a body in that kitchen, just like I know there's a body in the yard there. You can continue to resent me for having a gift I never asked for, but if you ignore what I'm saying now, you're the one who's going to look like an idiot when the press finds out you discovered one body in the backyard and never thought to search the house."

"Oh, we are searching that house," Mitchell says. "The second we find that body, we have an obligation to search that house for clues as to who did this."

"Wilson McDonald did this," Officer Andrews says.

"Then why is he dead?" I ask.

"You're the only one claiming he is." Officer Andrews crosses his arms, continuing to block my path into the house.

"Brennan, Andrews," Officer Wallace says, "we've got a body."

Mitchell pushes past Officer Andrews and grabs for the handle on the sliding glass door. Like I thought, it slides right open.

"The murderer couldn't lock the door behind him," I tell Officer Andrews. "Just in case you need help piecing this together. Feel free to take notes." I move around him to follow Mitchell inside.

The body is next to the kitchen island. The pool of blood by the victim's head indicates he was hit with a blunt object, cracking his skull. I look around, and my eyes land on a frying pan on the stove.

Officer Andrews walks into the house and curses.

"Believe me, I'm just as sorry as you are that I'm right." I hate finding dead bodies. "This happened recently," I say.

I'm sure Officer Wallace called the coroner once he found Amelia's body, so there's no reason to call this in, too. I walk around the island to the stove. We may need to lift fingerprints off the handle of the frying pan, so I can't exactly pick it up and read it right now. "I'm pretty sure this was the murder weapon," I say.

Officer Andrews beats Mitchell to me. "Don't touch it."

"I'm not an idiot." I meet Mitchell's gaze. "Once it's analyzed for prints, I'll need to read it. I can find out exactly who killed this guy."

"The prints will tell us that," Officer Andrews says.

"If there are any other than Wilson's." The killer we're dealing with is smart. He wouldn't be careless enough to touch the frying pan without gloves. Or if he was reacting in a heated moment, he'd at least think to wipe his prints off the handle with the dish towel.

Mitchell bends down to examine the body. "Who do you think this guy is? I mean, Amelia Crane is buried in his backyard, yet he can't be her killer."

"First of all, we don't have a clue who is in that backyard," Officer Andrews says. "Second, we have every reason to believe that Wilson McDonald did kill whoever it is."

"I suppose he hit himself over the head, put the frying pan back on the stove, and then walked back over to the island where he collapsed dead on the ground," I say. "Great theory, Officer."

"I want her out of here," he tells Mitchell. "She might be working the Spencer case, but there's no connection to either of these bodies, so she has no reason to be here."

"I wholeheartedly disagree," I say. "It's all the same killer."

"You have nothing to prove that. I want you out of here, Ashwell. Now."

Dad walks into the house and immediately glares at Officer Andrews. "Problem, Andrews?"

"Thomas, you aren't on the force anymore. You have no seniority over me."

If I didn't already love my father as much as humanly possible, I would now as he literally laughs in Officer Andrews's face.

"Kurt, the day I allow you to kick my daughter off a crime scene is the day it's *my* dead body being discovered. And even in that instance, I'd get my ghostly soul up out of my corpse and haunt your sorry ass for the rest of your life. Am I making myself clear?"

Mitchell clears his throat to cover up a laugh. He's been a bad influence on my father.

Even with Dad and Mitchell sticking up for my right to be here, I have no reason to hang around. I've already seen what I need to from this crime scene. What I do want is to read something that belonged to Wilson McDonald before I leave. I step out of the kitchen, letting the men work out this dispute without me. The garage is connected to the kitchen, so I slip in there without anyone noticing I'm gone. A black Lexus is parked in the center of the garage, and that will do just fine for me.

I walk over and place my hand on the door handle.

Wilson opens the car door, cell phone between his face and his shoulder. "I need to cancel my weekly appointment."

"May I ask the reason?" the woman on the other end of the line asks.

Wilson gets in the driver's seat, placing his briefcase on the seat beside him, and starts the engine. "My yard doesn't look any better than it did. It's been years, and I still have that wonky patch of grass in the back. You guys assured me they'd fix it, but they haven't and I pay too much to still be dealing with this problem."

When I open my eyes, Mitchell is standing next to me. I jump and place my hand on my chest. "You scared me."

"Sorry. I was trying not to disturb your vision. Did you see anything useful?"

"Wilson was talking to the landscaping company he

used. He was calling to cancel the service because he wasn't happy with his backyard."

"Well, I guess that means he didn't know about the dead body," Mitchell says.

"Agreed, but that can't be all my vision was trying to show me."

"Okay, then walk me through it. Maybe together we can figure out what you're missing." He leans on the front of the car and faces me.

"I didn't see anything else. He just called them and said he wanted to cancel his service. Maybe I should try to read the car again."

"Well, that might have to wait. I got a call from Chief Johansen. He wants all of us, you and your dad included, to come to the station. And the call came right after Andrews got off the phone with him."

"You don't think he's really going to try to bring trespassing charges against me, do you?"

"Honestly, I have no idea what this is about."

"All right. I'll go grab Dad and see you there then, I guess."

Mitchell starts to walk away but then turns back to me. "Don't forget we're supposed to look like a couple, so try not to roll your eyes at me too much while we're there."

I smirk and roll my eyes.

"Good idea. Get it out of your system now." He smiles and walks back into the kitchen.

I exit through the door on the side of the garage and

walk around to Dad's car. He's already inside it, waiting for me. "Ready to face the firing squad?" I ask him as I get in and click my seat belt into place.

"Are you kidding me?" Dad starts the engine and winks at me. "I'm not sure Chief Johansen is ready to face the Ashwells."

Thirty minutes later, I'm back at the Weltunkin PD despite my earlier assertion that I wouldn't meet with Chief Johansen. Officer Wallace is still at the crime scene with the rest of the CSI team, which means friendly faces are hard to come by. Not even Officer Gilbert is around.

Chief Johansen comes out of his office. "Andrews, you first," he says.

Officer Andrews walks past Mitchell and me with a smile on his face. Of course, he wants to tell his side of the story first. I'm sure he'll attempt to discredit anything Mitchell and I will say before we even get in there.

Mitchell and I sit down at his desk as we wait our turn. Dad, on the other hand, is drinking water by the water cooler as if this were any other day. I admire his composure. If only it would rub off on me the way people's anger tends to.

Fifteen minutes later, Officer Andrews walks out of the chief's office with a big grin on his face. "Your turn," he says to Mitchell and me.

"Ashwell," the chief yells, and Dad starts toward the office. "Just Piper," the chief adds.

Dad looks like he's going to storm in there anyway, but

I shake my head at him. I'm not about to let the chief think I need my daddy to fight my battles for me.

I walk into the office and sit down as if I don't have a concern in the world. "Afternoon, Chief."

"Ashwell, Andrews has informed me that you entered a property on a hunch without a warrant and without trying to contact the owner. Is that true?" His face is void of all emotion.

"Hmm, not exactly. I don't operate on 'hunches.'" I make air quotes. "My senses were drawn to that property because I've read something of Amelia Crane's. It was her that I sensed. Being that she's dead, I figured I should look into that."

"I see. And what did you do upon arriving at the property?" he asks, still showing zero emotion.

"Well, I figured ringing the doorbell of a possible killer probably wasn't the smartest idea, so my father called Detective Brennan to inform him of where we were and to request backup. I was drawn to the backyard, and after peeking over the fence, I noticed one area of grass looked healthier than the rest, as if it was being fertilized more. My senses zeroed in on that, so I had my father request Officer Wallace and Harry's assistance. It was then that Officer Andrews decided it was okay to check out the property. I can only speculate as to what changed his mind since he initially refused to come."

Chief Johansen leans back in his chair. "By all means, speculate."

"Okay, I believe Officer Andrews didn't trust my senses at first, but when Harry was asked to come confirm my suspicion, Officer Andrews decided he should be there to unearth the body in a case that was previously his."

"It still is his, Ms. Ashwell."

"Fair enough," I say.

"Please continue."

"While I was in the backyard, I sensed another body inside the house. That's when I realized we weren't at the killer's place of residence. We were merely at Amelia's burial site."

"What can you tell me about Wilson McDonald?"

It's clear Chief Johansen has already looked into McDonald and is testing me, which means I need to read a hell of a lot into that one small vision I had. "From what I saw, McDonald was a busy man. His job kept him away from home most of the time, which made it impossible for him to keep up with caring for his yard. Therefore, he hired a landscaper. The problem was that the landscapers couldn't seem to stop that one area in the backyard from growing more than the rest of the yard. After paying an astronomical fee every week for years, McDonald had enough and called to cancel the service."

"And how does McDonald tie into the case of Amelia Crane?"

I knew the question was going to come up, and I still don't have an answer. If Mitchell were in here with me—or Dad for that matter—we could possibly play the game to see what else my senses will reveal. But I'm on my own. Or am I? "Chief, I'd like to demonstrate something to you, but it will require your assistance."

"Go on."

"I need you to ask me a series of questions, starting with mundane things and working up to the question you just asked about McDonald and Crane."

"I'm not sure I understand."

"You don't have to. I just need you to ask me the questions. I promise it will make sense once we're through."

He sighs but sits forward and clasps his hands on his desk. "Okay, how old were you when you found out you had psychic abilities?"

I close my eyes. "Twelve."

"Was it scary working on the Belinda Maxwell case at that age?"

"Yes."

"Is Brennan a good detective?"

"Yes."

"Did you do something to make Officer Andrews so angry with you?"

"Yes."

"How does McDonald factor into the Crane case?"

"He's seen the killer."

"Was he working with him?"

"No."

"Were they friends?"

"No."

"Is there evidence in McDonald's house that will lead us to the killer?"

"Yes."

"Can you find it for me?"

"Yes."

"Are you really dating Brennan?"

I laugh and open my eyes. "I think we're finished here."

The chief cocks his head. "How do you do it?"

"I honestly don't know, Chief."

"I have one more question for you, Ms. Ashwell."

"Shoot." I'm feeling much more at ease with the chief now that he seems genuinely interested in my abilities.

He stares me right in the eye. "Should I request a transfer for Officer Andrews?"

CHAPTER THIRTEEN

I'm too stunned to answer at first. I never thought showing the chief a little of my abilities would make him come around in this way. Would he really transfer Officer Andrews because of me?

"Sir, I don't understand why you'd ask me that."

He stands up and walks to the window. "Ashwell, I know what people say about me around here. And I know I've given them a reason to believe I'm a hard-ass. But the truth is, I can admit when I'm wrong." He turns around to face me. "I was wrong about you, and that was largely in part of believing what Officer Andrews said told me."

"Like I said, I did do something to upset him. I was out of line, and he hasn't forgiven me." I can't believe I'm defending Officer Andrews right now, but the man's job is on the line.

"We aren't in middle school, Ms. Ashwell. We're

adults. You uncovered two dead bodies today. If not for you, we still wouldn't know the location of what appears to be Amelia Crane's remains. And we would have no knowledge of Wilson McDonald. So yes, I admit I misjudged you. I thought by putting you on this case, I'd watch you fail and prove Officer Andrews's theory that you simply get lucky sometimes. The problem is I don't believe Officer Andrews is capable of admitting the same."

"If I'm being honest, I don't think making him Mitchell's partner is a good idea. Partners have to have each other's backs, and those two don't even like each other."

He nods. "Point taken. As of this moment, Detective Brennan is free to work with whomever he wishes on future cases, including you, Ms. Ashwell."

"Thank you, sir." I'm almost afraid to ask. "What about Officer Andrews?"

"I'd like you to send him back in. You and I are finished here."

I'm stunned, but I stand up and start for the door.

"Oh, and Ms. Ashwell, to be clear, you are welcome on any and all cases Detective Brennan sees fit to bring to you."

I feel like I owe him something after his change of heart. "Chief, you should know Mitchell and I aren't dating. We're partners and friends."

"I thought you were both better detectives than that, but I suppose it's often most difficult to see the things that are directly in front of our faces." He waves his hand, dismissing me from the office.

I look at the floor until I reach Officer Andrews's desk. "The chief wants to see you," I say, and he must mistake my solemn tone for being upset after getting a verbal lashing, because Officer Andrews smiles all the way into the chief's office.

Since the door is wide open, we can hear everything the chief says.

"What the hell were you trying to pull, Andrews? You fed me purposely misleading information to try to get Ms. Ashwell removed from future cases. You've acted in a way that is unbecoming of an officer of this station."

"But, Chief—"

"Do I sound like I'm finished?" Chief Johansen bellows.

"No, sir," Officer Andrews says in the most subservient tone possible.

Without realizing it, I take a step toward the chief's office, but Mitchell holds me back.

"Don't, Piper. No matter what you do to try to save him, Andrews is never going to accept you. Besides, he's had this verbal lashing coming for a while. Just let this play out."

"You are hereby suspended for one month," Chief Johansen says. "During that time, you will return to the academy and review your training in the hopes that you can rediscover the officer that was hired by this station."

As much as I'm happy the chief respects what I do, I'm not happy that it's costing Officer Andrews his badge, even temporarily. I may not like the guy, but I don't want him getting suspended because of me.

He steps out of the chief's office, but his head isn't lowered like I'd think. He looks directly at me. "Happy now? You got what you wanted."

"I never wanted this." I hold out my hand. I wish I had enough control over my visions to read him and tell him everything will be okay, but my premonitions are still few and far between.

"Save it, Ashwell. Unlike everyone else here, I'm not buying your crap."

Chief Johansen steps out of his office. "Andrews, you're dismissed. Ashwell, both Ashwells actually, I want you and Brennan over at McDonald's house. Find me some evidence to link McDonald and the killer."

"You got it, Chief," Mitchell says, placing his hand on the small of my back.

"I told him the truth," I tell Mitchell. There's no reason to fake a relationship now that the chief actually wants me on this case.

"Oh." He lowers his hand. "Got it."

Dad hangs back to have a word with the chief, and Mitchell and I head to the patrol car. "Let's take Dad's car," I say. "I do not want to ride in the back seat of a police car. It makes me feel like a criminal."

Mitchell smirks. "I bet Andrews would get a kick out of seeing you back there."

I look across the parking lot to Officer Andrews. He's on the phone, most likely calling for a ride since he can't use the patrol car while he's suspended. "I hate this. It's only going to make things worse between us."

"It was never going to get better, Piper. Not with a guy like Andrews. You could have helped him solve every case and let him take all the credit, and he'd still treat you the way he does. He's jealous of you because you can do what he can't. Plain and simple."

I stare across the roof of the car at Mitchell. If anyone has a reason to be jealous of what I do, it's Mitchell, yet he's never held it against me. "Why don't you hate me?"

He laughs. "Really, Piper, I thought you'd figured me out by now."

"I don't think I'll ever have you figured out." Mitchell isn't like anyone else I've ever met. He's kind of a walking contradiction. More so, he's changed so much in the short time I've known him.

Dad emerges from the station and heads toward Mitchell's patrol car instead of his own. "Ready?"

I decide to throw Officer Andrews a bone and let him see me in the back of the patrol car instead of insisting Dad drives. I do my best to put on a look of despair as we drive by him. Mitchell, being Mitchell, honks his horn and waves.

"Don't," I tell him. "The guy is being punished enough."

"You've got to be kidding me," Mitchell says. "How can you stand up for him after all he's put you through?"

"Actually, I agree with Piper," Dad says. "That's what I was talking to the chief about. Andrews has an ego, and yes, that's a problem, but this isn't the solution. I think he had a better idea when he forced the three of you to work together."

"We'd kill each other," Mitchell and I both say, earning us a look from Dad.

"You'd have a common goal to focus on, and since you're all professionals, you wouldn't let personal business interfere with solving a case."

Sure, if Mitchell, Andrews, and I were as mature and reasonable as Dad. We're clearly not. "What did the chief say?" I ask, hoping he didn't agree with Dad.

"He's going to let Andrews analyze some cold cases while he's suspended. Basically, just using his insight on possible leads. That way he's still technically working but he's not out in the field."

Chief Johansen does have a softer side. "Thanks, Dad," I say.

Mitchell just shakes his head. "So, what do you think we'll find at McDonald's place?"

"Well, the killer had to have access to the property in order to bury Amelia without McDonald knowing." It was something I didn't want to voice to the chief. "I think he might have been part of the original landscaping crew." It would explain why I had that particular vision of McDonald.

"That would be the perfect disguise," Dad says. "It gives him access to the property while McDonald isn't home."

"Exactly. But I think he quit shortly after that, if not right away. He wouldn't want to stick around."

"But that means someone at the landscaping company would know the killer's name and what he looks like," Mitchell says.

"Fake name and disguise," I say, knowing it's true.

"Easy enough to pull off," Dad says.

"That means anything you see in a vision would show the killer in disguise and under a fake name," Mitchell continues. "How do we find him then?"

"Has anyone checked in at the prison to make sure O'Neil is still being supervised at all times?" I ask, suddenly worried about his safety again.

"This morning, I called a contact I have there," Dad says. "O'Neil is still in solitary, and he has a guard assigned specifically to him."

"What's the guard's name? We need to check him out to make sure he's not connected to our killer in any way."

Mitchell eyes me in the rearview mirror. "And how exactly do we do that when we have no idea who the killer is?"

"You always have to ask the difficult questions, don't you?" I lean back against the seat.

"The guard watching him is Lucy Romero," Dad says. "She's tough, and she's been there for about twenty years now."

I run the name through my mind, hoping to get something about Romero, but I come back with a big fat nothing.

McDonald's house looks like your typical crime scene. Mitchell opens my door for me, which makes me feel like a hardened criminal. But I immediately pick up on something when I step out of the car. This time, we're parked in the driveway instead of the street. I've already been inside the garage, so what is it I'm sensing? It can't be anything in there.

I take a few steps toward the house.

"What are you sensing?" Mitchell asks me.

"I'm not sure yet."

"Just follow it, pumpkin. Let it lead you," Dad says, and I know he's not just saying this for my benefit. He's trying to tell Mitchell not to interfere or interrupt with questions.

I move toward the garage and stop. I place my hand on the door, but I immediately sense that's not right. I step to the side so the right side of the house is in view. There's an access door to a crawl space. Going to it, I bend down and inspect the latch. It's not locked, which means anyone could have opened it. I give Dad and Mitchell a brief look before placing my right hand on the handle and closing my eyes.

It's dark, but the sounds of a lawnmower and a weedwhacker fill the air. The sunlight coming through the small crevice where the door closes is just enough to illuminate a watch on a thin wrist. 2:14.

I open my eyes. "He was here. As in down there." I pull open the door to reveal a four-foot tall space that appears to run about half the length of the house.

"Back away, Piper," Mitchell says, gun drawn. "I'm going in there first."

"He's not here anymore," I assert, already stepping down into the space.

"Do you ever listen?" he asks, following me inside the crawl space.

"I thought you knew me by now," I say, using his own words against him.

"Very funny."

The crawl space appears to be an access to the grinder pump. Luckily, it's functioning properly because there's no odor down here. The rest of the space is completely empty, making it a good hiding spot for the killer while he waited out the landscapers.

"I was wrong. He didn't work with the landscapers. He was using them to cover up for burying the body."

"How though?" Mitchell asks. "He'd still have to dig up the backyard."

"Not if the landscapers already intended to do so,"

Dad says, joining us in the crawl space. "I did some digging of my own just now."

I smirk at Dad. "You called pretending to be McDonald," I say.

Dad feigns being appalled. "I'd never impersonate a dead man. I said I was his brother and I was taking care of closing Wilson's accounts. I asked for an explanation of services rendered so far under the guise of needing to know for the resale of the home."

"Smart," Mitchell says.

"A French drain was installed in the backyard to prevent a flooding issue caused by an underground stream. The yard was already dug up for that."

"Let me guess," I say. "They replaced the grass with sod, which the killer just had to lift and then dig far enough to bury the body."

"And then he recovered the spot with the sod," Mitchell says.

"Bingo." Dad wipes his palms together in the gesture that means something is finished.

"Okay, so we know how he did it. But how then, did he know McDonald to find out he was having this work done?" That's what we need to figure out. Right now, we have no connection between anyone involved.

"Let's go inside and look around," Mitchell says. "I think we've gotten all we can from this space."

Dad and I both give him a look at the word "we."

"You know what I mean," he says, waving us out of the crawl space.

"We're teasing, Mitchell. We all came up with ideas down there." I brush the dirt off my pants as I step back onto the grass. "Is the back door still open?" I ask.

"To my knowledge," Mitchell says, and we start around back.

I know this search is most likely going to be me reading everything and anything to find a connection between McDonald and the killer. McDonald was chosen by this guy, but how would the killer know McDonald was having yardwork done if they didn't know each other? That doesn't make sense. The connection exists. I just have to find it.

I walk through the kitchen, noticing the frying pan is gone. It's evidence in the murder investigation. Evidence I'll read later. I allow my senses to lead me. Dad and Mitchell know better than to interfere with my process. I go to the living room just off the kitchen. Something in the corner makes me stop dead in my tracks. Not because it's covered by a sheet and almost looks like the form of a human is hiding underneath it. But because I know exactly what it is. My senses are tingling, sending goose bumps popping up along my arms and legs.

"Piper," Mitchell stops beside me, his gaze glued to the exact object that has all of my attention. "Is that what I think it is?"

I nod, take a deep breath, and move toward the object.

I'm not being completely honest with Mitchell because he doesn't know the extent to which this object connects McDonald to Amelia Crane. I stop just before it and then yank off the sheet.

"That's the exact same bird cage Amelia Crane had," Mitchell says.

CHAPTER FOURTEEN

It's a perfect match to the bird cage now located in Mitchell's living room. From the pedestal to the curved cage, the details are identical. The only difference is the bird inside. Amelia's bird is still alive. McDonald's is lying dead on the bottom of the cage. O'Neil's words ring through my head: "Dead women can still talk, but a dead bird can't sing."

"Dead birds can't sing," I say in a low tone.

"Someone want to fill me in?" Dad asks, his hands in his pockets as he observes our reactions to this bird cage.

"This cage is identical to the one we retrieved from Hilltop House. The one that formerly belonged to Amelia Crane. It's currently in my living room in case Piper needs to read it again to solve the case." Mitchell reaches for the latch on the cage, which is broken. "Someone killed this bird."

"But why?" I ask. And before anyone else can respond, the answer presents itself to me. "The bird could talk. More than Amelia's could, so the killer had to shut it up."

"A dead bird can't sing," Mitchell says. "How did O'Neil know this?"

I'm starting to think O'Neil wasn't so innocent in Amelia's murder after all. "He wants us to find his accomplice, but it's not because he's innocent. It's because O'Neil is tired of serving time for this crime alone. He really was stalking her. I think he developed a crush on her along the way, but he still intended to follow through with her murder."

"Are you saying he played us?" Mitchell asks. "I actually was starting to think he was an innocent man."

"You and me both. I misread the signs, though. O'Neil is guilty. He's not going to willingly give up his accomplice, but he's not afraid of him either. He wanted the credit for killing Amelia." The sick bastard. "But I think he's also hoping that by helping us find the second guilty party, he might get out of prison before he dies."

Mitchell rakes a hand through his hair. "We have to go back to that prison, don't we?"

"Tomorrow," I say. "I definitely want to talk to O'Neil again, but right now I'm going to read this bird cage because O'Neil had that all wrong. The dead bird can talk to me, and I intend to listen to what it has to say."

I'm no stranger to reading animals, but this would be

the first dead animal I've ever read. I open the latch on the cage.

"Piper, wait." Mitchell places his hand on mine and lowers my arm. "I have another idea." He reaches inside the cage and pulls a single feather from the bottom. "Here," he says. "This is easier to take with us, and this way you don't have to touch the dead bird."

"Good thinking," I say, taking the feather from him in my left hand. I move to the couch and sit down. After taking several deep breaths, I transfer the feather to my right hand.

"I have the paperwork in my briefcase. I would have brought it to you, though."

"I was in the area, so I figured I'd save you the trip."

"That was thoughtful of you—"

A loud thud with a slight metallic ring to it fills the air, and the bird squawks, "Come in."

"Stupid bird." The voice is closer.

"Stupid bird," the bird echoes.

"Dead bird," the man says.

"Dead—"

I open my eyes. "Damn it." Why my visions are sometimes just sounds, I'll never know. It wasn't like it was nighttime or even dark in the house when this happened. Or maybe it was. I'm not sure since I couldn't see anything.

"What is it, pumpkin?" Dad asks. "What did you see?"

"Nothing. I heard McDonald and the killer talking."

"What did they say?" Mitchell asks, sitting down beside me on the couch.

"McDonald had some paperwork for him. The killer said he was here to get it, but really, he came to kill McDonald. I heard him hit McDonald over the head with the frying pan."

"So they were in business together, then." Mitchell nods. "This is good. We'll look into McDonald's business contacts.

"Anything else?" Dad asks. He knows the bird has to come into play somehow since I read the feather.

And then it dawns on me. "The bird." My eyes go to the sheet I removed from the bird cage. "I couldn't see anything in the vision because the sheet was over the cage. The bird couldn't see anything."

"Your vision was from the bird's perspective?" Mitchell asks.

"Apparently. The bird heard the slight ringing sound the frying pan made when it connected with McDonald's head, and it must have thought it was the doorbell or something because it said, 'Come in.'"

"And that drew the killer to the bird," Dad says.

"Exactly. And when the killer talked to the bird, it repeated what he said."

"Which made the killer realize the bird was a witness and could possibly talk," Mitchell says.

"So he killed it." Even though I didn't witness that part

of the vision, the phantom pain in my neck tells me the killer snapped the bird's neck.

"All right," Dad says, "let's reconvene tomorrow in the office. We'll get a list of people McDonald worked with and go from there."

He's right. The entire day has gotten away from me yet again. I'm starving and exhausted.

After dropping Dad off at his car and telling him to give Jez a kiss for me, we head to Mitchell's condo.

"You know, you can bring Jez here if you'd like. I feel bad that you didn't even get to see her today."

It's not a bad idea, but at my parents' house, Jez can play with Max, and she has Mom to walk and feed her. "I think she's better off where she is, but thanks for the offer."

"I'm going to order pizza to be delivered."

"Great, can we swing by my apartment so I can grab a change of clothes?"

"Sure." He makes a quick turn to change directions.

An hour later, I'm showered and in yoga pants and a T-shirt when Mitchell's doorbell rings.

"I got it," he calls from the kitchen. He rushes to the door, money in hand.

When he returns with the pizza boxes and paper plates, he puts them on the coffee table.

"No wonder your coffee table has so many rings on it. Not only do you put drinks here without coasters, you put hot food directly on top of the wood," I say, sitting forward and opening the top box.

"Hey, I grew up without a mother. What do you expect?" His tone is sad, and I instantly regret saying anything.

I take a slice of sausage pizza and close the box, knowing Mitchell will want a slice of pepperoni instead.

He's staring at me awkwardly as he sits down on the floor on the other side of the coffee table. "Why are you looking at me like that?"

"I was about to ask you the same." I put my plate on my lap before taking a big bite of pizza.

"You have this strange look on your face. I can't place it."

After swallowing, I say, "I just noticed that your T-shirt is clinging to you in several spots, which means you didn't dry off well after your shower. And your hair needs to be trimmed."

He laughs. "I haven't exactly had time to get my hair cut, and I was in a hurry to get dressed before the pizza arrived. Anything else, Ms. Ashwell?"

I bite my lower lip and cock my head at him. "Yes, actually. You're sitting on the floor. You poured yourself both water and iced tea." I squint my eyes at him. "And there's something on your mind, but you don't know how to say it."

"Perceptive. I wanted iced tea, but it's a diuretic and I haven't had any water all day."

I nod. "Okay, makes sense. Go on."

"I'm sitting on the floor because the bird hates me and

flung birdseed at me all last night. He prefers when we keep our distance."

I laugh. "Well, it's possible Amelia didn't have male visitors. Or maybe the bird just doesn't like men."

"Maybe."

"You saved the best for last. What's on your mind, Detective?" I take another bite of my pizza.

"I want you to teach me to open myself up to my intuition."

"Oh." I wasn't expecting that. I probably should have, seeing as how Mitchell's pondered why he didn't get his mother's ability. "Why now?"

"I don't think you should have to go through all the hard stuff on your own."

I lower my head, focusing on a single piece of sausage on my pizza. "I don't. I have my dad and you to help me through it."

"You know what I mean. We can comfort you after a bad vision, but you're always the one who has to have them. It's a lot of pressure on one person. It doesn't seem fair."

More like he doesn't think it's fair that I can see these things and he can't. "Mitchell, you know what happened to my grandmother and your mom." I swallow hard when Mitchell's face falls. "If I'm being honest, most days I wish I didn't have this ability."

He raises his head to meet my gaze. "What do you think your life would be like if you didn't?"

I've thought about that a lot, but it's hard to imagine since the things I'd most likely have are things I've never experienced. Like love. A real relationship. "What do you think your life would be like if you did have your mother's clairvoyance?" I counter.

"Don't avoid the question, Piper." Mitchell's voice is stern, letting me know he's not allowing me to get off the hook that easily. "Talk to me."

"You know, we became friends because neither one of us did emotions well. Why are you changing the rules of our relationship?"

"What exactly is our relationship?" he asks.

"Friends. Partners. Colleagues." I shrug and look at my pizza again, no longer hungry.

"If I had my mom's gift, I think I'd be more like you, and maybe you wouldn't push me away so much. Maybe you'd welcome the idea of being with me because I'd understand exactly what you go through with your visions." He blurts it all out in one breath.

"Or we'd both be such basket cases we wouldn't be able to be around each other at all."

"When you met Sam, you were excited about the prospect of being friends with another psychic."

"Friends, Mitchell. That's the key word there. And Sam Pierce is probably the worst example ever considering he tried to kill me."

Mitchell clears his throat. "You know what? I think we should probably get back to the case."

"Good idea." I take a deep breath.

"Let's play the game," he suggests, putting his plate on the floor, not having eaten any of his pizza.

I shrug and place my pizza on the table. The game is probably our best bet right now anyway.

"Okay, ready?"

I close my eyes and take a deep breath before nodding.

"What's Amelia's bird's name?" Mitchell begins.

"Jeffrey."

"How was Wilson McDonald murdered?"

"With a frying pan."

"What object did you read in McDonald's house?"

"A feather?"

"Do I have any shot at a relationship with you?"

"Yes." My eyes snap open, and I jump to my feet. I can't believe he'd do something like that to me. He knows I can only speak the truth when I'm in my meditative state. I was vulnerable to anything he asked, and he chose to take advantage of it. "That was way out of line."

"You're right. I'm sorry." He stands, holding his hands up in surrender.

"I don't think you are. You set me up. That's why you suggested playing the game in the first place, isn't it?" I shake my head at him, and tears form in my eyes. "Damn it, Mitchell. You had no right."

"You didn't have a right to read me against my will when we met, either. If you hadn't, you might not have the same opinion of me you do now."

I'm so angry I'm shaking. "You're dead wrong. When I met you, I thought you were a pig, dating random women all the time, and I was right. But I also know you aren't that person anymore. I know how much you've grown. I never would have even thought you were the kind of person I could..." My voice shakes, and I stop.

"You could what, Piper?" He moves toward me and takes my hands in his.

"Don't." I jerk my hands away as I turn my back to him. "You can't keep doing this, Mitchell. You say you're fine with the way things are between us, but you keep pushing me."

"I've pushed you from day one because if I don't, you'll revert back to shutting me out. You have to see that you do that, Piper."

A tear slips down my cheek, and I brush it away before saying, "I'm tired. I'm going to bed."

He doesn't stop me as I push past him and head to the bedroom.

CHAPTER FIFTEEN

I wake up insanely early and call Uber to avoid having to drive to the office with Mitchell. I don't want to be around him at all right now. I've let my guard down with him so much, but instead of giving me credit for it, he continues to push me. He totally disrespected my right to privacy and tricked me into admitting I have feelings for him. My answer even surprised me, because as aware as I am about my feelings, I didn't think it would result in a relationship with him. I guess I don't even know myself sometimes.

Instead of going to my office, I knock on the door of Marcia's Nook. It's too early to be open, but I know Marcia is there baking. It takes a little while before she sees me. I could have called her, but I'm not exactly thinking clearly.

"You look terrible," she says, opening the door for me. "What happened?"

"Mitchell." As much as I don't want to rehash what happened, I need another perspective on this, and since my mother loves Mitchell, I know what she'll say. And talking to my dad would be more than awkward.

"Come on. I'll get you some coffee, and you can tell me all about it while I make muffins." She pours me a large toasted almond coffee and brings me to the kitchen in the back, where she resumes mixing batter. "Tell me what he did."

I never told Marcia that Mitchell kissed me on a previous case when I was in the middle of a complete mental breakdown. I decide to lay it all out there.

"So the stupid idiot thought kissing me was the way to stop me from totally losing it."

Marcia stops pouring the batter and stares at me. "It probably had the complete opposite effect."

I nod. "Then he asked me to read him after that, and I witnessed a conversation he had with my father. He told him how he feels about me." I raise a hand to my forehead. "I don't know if I was more embarrassed my dad knows or if I'm angry that Mitchell would bring him into this."

"I'm sure it's both." She wipes her hands on her apron and walks over to me. "Sweetie, that man is not good with women. We both know that. But I think his heart is in the right place, especially where you're concerned. I've told you for months that all he talks about when he comes in here is you."

There was a time when I thought Mitchell and Marcia

were secretly dating, until she clued me in on the fact that I was the only thing they ever talked about.

"What am I going to do about him? I actually got to a point where I liked being around him."

She reaches for my left hand and takes it between both of hers. "You can't fault him for being crazy about you. Yes, he's acting like an idiot, but he's a man." She laughs. "Worse, he's a man who fell for the one woman who can see every one of his discretions. That can't be easy for him, yet he still wants to make this work."

"Tell me what to do."

She smiles and waves me out of the kitchen. "You go sit down, drink your coffee, and try not to think so much. Sometimes you just have to let life happen."

We walk back out to the café seating area, and I spy Mitchell standing outside the door. I turn to face Marcia.

"Your call," she says. "I don't open for another thirty minutes."

"You'd leave him standing out there?" I ask.

She bobs one shoulder. "It would give him time to think about what he's done. Or you could talk to him. I'll leave it to you. I have muffins to finish making." She disappears back inside the kitchen.

I sigh as I stare at Mitchell with his hands in his pockets, looking completely lost. That's not the Mitchell Brennan who flirts mercilessly with countless women. I walk over and unlock the door for him, but I don't open it. We stand there for a minute, staring at each other through the glass door in silence. Then he reaches for the doorknob and comes inside the store.

"I want to yell at you and apologize all at the same time, and I have no idea how to do that," he says.

I sip my coffee. "Need some caffeine to jumpstart your brain?" I start toward the bakery counter. I once helped Marcia serve customers when the place was packed, and I don't think she'd object to me pouring coffee for Mitchell, so I do just that.

He leans on the counter and waves to Marcia in the kitchen.

"Morning, Detective," she says, placing the tray of muffins into the oven. Even though I suspect she's finished baking for the time being, she doesn't leave the kitchen to join us.

"Here you go." I hand Mitchell the coffee and rest my forearms on the countertop.

"Can we sit and talk?" He motions to a table behind him.

"Sure." I walk around the counter and sit down across from him at the table.

"I panicked when I woke up and you were gone. Nice job turning off your cell phone so I couldn't call you."

I nod and take another sip of coffee.

"You do realize you're a target in this case. The killer specifically knows about you. He had Hugo Spencer watch you."

"I get it." Calling Uber was stupid on my part. I could

have wound up in a car with the killer if he was watching me closely enough. "I'll apologize for that."

Mitchell takes a deep breath and then a sip of coffee before saying, "I'm sorry for the stunt I pulled. It was probably the stupidest thing I could have done. I've worked hard to gain your trust, and I ruined it all in a second."

I trust Mitchell with my life. I'm just not sure I trust him with my heart. "Look, we have a case we need to solve, so why don't we table this for now."

"There's always going to be a case, Piper."

"Yeah, and I'm always going to have these abilities that make things harder for me to deal with, and you're always going to do things that piss me off. What else is new?"

He smirks. "Yet you actually like me. It's kind of astonishing." His green eyes almost sparkle in the lighting of the café, and I have to avert my gaze.

"I had a dream last night."

"About me?" he asks.

I roll my eyes. "About the case. Specifically the bird cages. There were two identical cages and two birds."

"Right." He narrows his eyes at me, not sure where I'm going with this.

"The only clue O'Neil gave me was about the birds. Two of them and one dead woman. But so far, all of my visions have been about one man or the other: the killer or O'Neil. Never both, yet I'm sure O'Neil tipped me off about the killer because he wants him to serve time, too."

"A jailbird in the vision is worth two in the prison," Mitchell says in a singsong way.

I shake my head and sigh. "How do you do that for every single case we work on?"

"It's a talent. One of many." He wags his eyebrows at me.

"Well, it would help if one of those talents was solving this case."

He puts his coffee on the table, laces his fingers, and turns his palms out to crack each and every knuckle. "All right. We can do this. The two identical cages could be a coincidence. It doesn't mean Amelia and McDonald knew each other. But we do know the killer knew McDonald."

"And both the killer and O'Neil knew Amelia."

"Right. But how?"

I bite my bottom lip as I think it over. "She was an actress, so it's possible they saw her perform."

"That would still make her a random target, though."

"True, but O'Neil couldn't have known her on a more personal level or she would have called him by name in the vision I had of her talking to her bird. She didn't know who he was other than he seemed to be following her around."

Mitchell taps his finger on the tabletop. "Then it's possible the killer knew Amelia, and O'Neil was hired to abduct her."

"It would be easier for someone she knew to abduct her."

"Unless..." Mitchell snaps his fingers. "Okay, maybe this is crazy hypothesizing, but what if O'Neil stalked Amelia so she'd be scared and run right to the actual killer?"

Yes. "Mitchell, that's it! You figured it out. My senses confirmed it the minute the words left your mouth." I could kiss him right now. Or not. Definitely not.

He sits back in his seat. "Is this what it feels like?" He raises his gaze to mine. "When things just come to you as truths, I mean."

I smile. He's so desperate to have these abilities. "I'd imagine what you're feeling is very similar. Yes."

"I don't know how you're not elated when this happens."

"For some reason, I'm finding it a whole lot more impressive when you do it."

He smiles. "Thanks." He wraps his fingers around his coffee cup. "Are we sure O'Neil is safe in prison now?"

"Sure? No. The killer knows O'Neil talked to us, but I'm not convinced he'd go anywhere near the prison or even contact anyone else there. He killed Hugo Spencer. If he went anywhere near O'Neil now, he'd be putting himself at great risk of being caught."

"Even still, I say we leave O'Neil in solitary until we solve this case."

"Agreed." It's one less thing for us to worry about. Although, I don't think I'd lose too much sleep if the man responsible for aiding in Amelia Crane's abduction was killed by the man he aided.

"What do you think Amelia's aunt and uncle have to do with all this?" Mitchell asks.

"Other than happily collecting her money, I'm not sure they're involved. They were crappy guardians, which is why Amelia left, but I don't think they hired someone to kill her."

"How do we proceed from here?"

"Can I see the frying pan used to kill Hugo Spencer?"

Mitchell cocks his head at me. "Are you sure you want to do that? You'd most likely see him being killed. And there's a really good chance you'd see the vision from the killer's perspective. We have other items for you to read."

He knows how being the killer in a vision can affect me. "All right. Let's save that as a last resort. I think I should try reading the bird cage again. Amelia's."

"Are you trying to get me to invite you over?" he asks with a sly smile.

"Yes. I fled your apartment this morning before you woke up because I wanted to trick you into inviting me over to your place."

His face falls. "I guess that doesn't make sense."

"No, not in the least." I stand up. "Let's grab some food and go pick up my dad. He should come with us." As a chaperone so Mitchell behaves himself for once.

Marcia walks out of the kitchen at the same time I

approach the bakery counter. "Here you go." She holds up a bakery box. "I thought you could use some crumb cake fresh out of the oven. I'll get you a refill on the coffees as well. One for your dad too, right?" She's rambling, which can only mean she was eavesdropping on our conversation.

"Yes, please." I let it slide since I know she's only looking out for me and was probably trying to be prepared if Mitchell did something that required her to intervene on my behalf.

Mitchell and I place our coffee cups on the counter, and she refills them after pouring Dad's. Mitchell has his wallet out, but I hold up my hand to stop him since he bought the pizza last night. I use my phone to pay. Mitchell places a ten-dollar bill in the tip jar, which makes Marcia scowl.

"At least he stopped tipping with twenties and fifties," I tell her. "There might be some hope for him yet."

She shakes her head as we walk out.

Jezebel greets us when we get to Mom and Dad's house. "I've never seen her whine like this in my life," I tell Mom.

"Well, she certainly missed you. I think she was worried you weren't coming back."

I hug her to my chest. "You poor baby. I'm so sorry." After her former owner never returned home, I can't blame Jez for thinking the same would happen to me. I pull back and hold her face in my hands. "I'm never going to leave you for good, you hear me?"

Mitchell bends down beside me and scratches her head. "You're stuck with me, too."

Jez licks him straight up the center of his face, making us all laugh.

Mitchell stands up. "If you'll excuse me, I'm going to go wash my face."

Mom watches him walk away before turning to me. "How is pretend dating going?"

"That's over," I say, standing up. "The chief is fully on my side now, so I told him the truth."

"Uh-huh." Mom's tone isn't lost on me.

"Is Dad ready yet?" I ask, changing the subject.

"That I am," he says, buttoning his shirt sleeve as he walks down the stairs.

"Good. I need to have a vision and get this case solved already."

"The funeral for Hugo Spencer is tomorrow," Mom says. "Are you three going?"

I hadn't thought about it, but it might not be a bad idea. We'd get more of a sense of who knew him, and that might lead us to the killer. "Yeah," I say. "I think it could help the case."

Dad opens the front door and kisses Mom goodbye, but his gaze is focused on me. Once we're outside, after reassuring Jez I would come back, Dad says, "You think the killer will show up at the funeral."

"Maybe not in the crowd," I say, opening the car door. "But I have a feeling he'll be lurking nearby."

"Does that mean we're lurking as well?" Mitchell asks as he starts the car.

"No. We'll be in full view with the mourners. Listening in on every conversation to see what we can find out."

We're all silent until we get to Mitchell's. Dad's been to Mitchell's condo before, but he looks around as if it's the first time he's seeing it, and it doesn't take me long to figure out why. "Oh my God," I whisper to him when Mitchell goes into the kitchen to get plates for Marcia's crumb cake. "You're trying to figure out if..." I can't even say it. "Mitchell sleeps on the couch, Dad."

Dad holds up his hands. "I'm just making sure he's being a gentleman. That's a father's job."

I huff as I walk over to the bird cage. "Good morning, Jeffrey. T.G.I.F."

The bird whistles in response.

"He does like to whistle," Mitchell says, returning with the plates and a knife. "I got up to use the bathroom in the middle of the night, and he whistled at me. Let me tell you, it's a little startling when you're half asleep."

"That's what you get for forgetting to cover his cage," I say. Something about my own words makes my senses tingle. I raise my hand and touch the cage.

Amelia's phone is pressed to her ear. "He was here again. Outside my apartment. I think I should go to the police." Amelia twists a lock of hair around her finger and stares at Jeffrey's cage. "I'm scared. I don't want to be another statistic."

She reaches one hand toward the cage and touches the top of Jeffrey's head. "I think I'll leave Jeffrey's cage uncovered tonight. At least if anyone tries to get in, he'll whistle at them." She gives a nervous laugh. "His whistle is so loud it's ear-piercing. It will scare the guy and wake me up."

She leans toward the cage. "Isn't that right, Jeffrey?"

Jeffrey whistles in response and then turns his head for a better scratch.

"I'll be there right after rehearsal, barring no incidents with my stalker. But seriously, if he doesn't stop soon, I'm going to call the police."

The vision ends, and I lower my hand.

"What did you see, pumpkin?" Dad asks.

I turn to face Mitchell. "You were right. She knew the killer. I'm pretty sure I just witnessed her talking to him on the phone."

"What makes you say that? Did you hear him?" Dad asks.

"No. It's just a feeling I have. Plus, she was telling the person on the other end of the call that her stalker was scaring her so much she wanted to go to the police, and the person on the other end seemed to be trying to talk her out of it."

I take a deep breath before saying the next part. "I

think the vision was from the night she died. She had plans to meet up with the killer."

CHAPTER SIXTEEN

"I can't believe I was right about this," Mitchell says, sitting down on the couch.

"Why? You're a great detective, Mitchell. I've told you all along that you don't give yourself enough credit on these cases. If I weren't here, you'd still figure things out."

"Not nearly as quickly, and some of these cases have been so crazy I'm not sure I would have ever solved them by myself."

Dad's gaze volleys between us. He raises his hands to interrupt the conversation. "First I have to referee because you two couldn't get along. Now I have to stop the onslaught of pats on the backs? I can't keep up."

"I need to know who Amelia hung out with. Who her friends were. Who her coworkers were. Everyone," I say.

"Well, we know she performed at the local theater. Let's start there," Mitchell says.

I nod. "Good. That's good." I turn to Dad. "Any chance you're willing to hang back and look more into Amelia's online presence? This person could have contacted her there and left a trail." Dad loves research of any kind, so I know he'll be game.

"Drop me off at the office on the way."

With a plan in place, we quickly scarf down some crumb cake and the rest of our coffee before heading out.

"Are you positive the Crane's aren't involved?" Mitchell asks once we've dropped off Dad and are headed to the theater.

"Why does it seem like you want them to be?" I stretch out my legs, happy to be in the passenger seat and not in the back behind those cage-like bars. I was feeling like a jailbird myself back there.

"I don't. They just struck me as awful people."

"Well, you're not wrong there. But my radar isn't picking up on them being behind this."

Mitchell finds a parking spot right in front of the theater since it's early morning and it's not even open for the day. "What are they odds anyone will be here?" he asks, getting out of the car.

"Let's go around back," I say, assuming that anyone in charge probably has an office back there and wouldn't park up front.

We walk around the side of the building, and I note the basement window. It would be easy enough for someone to hide down there. I'm sure the stage has a trap door for props and such, but neither O'Neil nor the killer hid from Amelia. O'Neil was the decoy, the distraction that made Amelia run right into the killer's arms.

"Any chance she was dating this guy?" Mitchell asks as if he was just reading my mind. It's a little freaky how he seems to know what I'm thinking at times. Yet other times he's so completely oblivious.

"Maybe. Amelia must have been friends with some of her fellow cast members, so if she was dating anyone, they'd know."

We arrive at a door on the back of the building, and I raise my hand to knock. Mitchell places his hands on his hips. To anyone else, it might seem like he's impatient for someone to open the door, but I know he's keeping his hand close to his gun just in case.

A woman with long dark hair peppered with gray streaks answers the door. I hesitate, expecting Mitchell to fall into his obnoxious flirting routine, but he stays silent.

"Hello, I'm Piper Ashwell, and this is Detective Brennan with the Weltunkin PD. We were hoping to speak with whomever is in charge about a former actress named Amelia Crane."

The woman puts her hand to her chest. "Amelia. I haven't thought about her in years." She shakes her head. "I admit I'm confused, though. She died, and her murderer is in prison. What could you possibly be investigating after all this time?"

"Ma'am, we've recently uncovered evidence that

suggests there were two men involved in Ms. Crane's murder," Mitchell says.

"Oh, how dreadful. And what exactly brings you here to my theater?" She still blocking the doorway, not allowing us inside, which makes me suspicious. Yet Amelia told the killer she'd meet him after rehearsal, so I don't think it was anyone connected to this theater. I'm just hoping someone here knew who he was.

"We just have a few questions for you. May we come inside?" I ask.

She finally steps back, allowing us into her office. "My staff will arrive within the hour, and I really don't want to start a mass hysteria. Theater types can be..."

"Dramatic?" Mitchell offers.

The woman smiles. "I was going to say theatrical. Much nicer word." She motions for us to take a seat, and she does the same. It's not your typical office. Sure, there's a desk and rolling desk chair, but there's also a red couch and chaise lounge. The woman actually sprawls out on the lounge chair. Mitchell and I exchange glances and sit on the couch.

My initial reaction to this woman is she's very theatrical herself. She's putting on a show and not at all acting how she typically would. She's playing a role. "Ms...." I pause, waiting for her to supply her name.

"Delila Herschel," she says.

Fake. Well, that's interesting. "You use a stage name," I say.

Mitchell's head whips in my direction, his pad and pen now in hand. "That's not her real name?" he asks me as if she's not sitting directly across from us.

"No. Why don't you use your real name?" I ask her.

She laughs. "It's not uncommon for people to use pseudonyms nowadays. Authors, actors..." She waves a hand in the air as if the list goes on and on despite the fact that she only provided two answers.

"I see. Well, since this is a murder investigation, perhaps you could give us your real name."

Mitchell is ready to scribble it down.

Delila sits up and huffs. "Fine." Her voice is suddenly two octaves lower than it was. "My first name is Delila, but my last name is Smith. You don't get more mundane than that, so I'm sure you can see why I opted to change it."

Makes sense I suppose. "And how well did you know Amelia?" I continue.

"She got the lead in a few plays and was the understudy in a few others. She was talented. Not talented enough to make it in say Hollywood or on Broadway, but for a local girl, she was good."

"Did you notice her bringing any men around the theater?" Mitchell asks.

Delila laughs. "Amelia brought lots of friends around here. Men and women. But that man that was arrested for her murder..." Delila swallows hard and takes a deep breath before continuing. "He was here for every one of her performances. Even when she was the understudy and never stepped foot on stage, he was front and center."

"Why didn't Amelia go to the police if she thought that man was stalking her?" I ask, hoping Delila might have a clue as to who told Amelia not to pursue help from the police.

"I don't know. One day, she'd come in here all in a huff talking about how scared she was. Then the next, she waved it off as no big deal. I told you. Some of these actors are very theatrical."

Ironic coming from the woman who just tried to act her way through this questioning. "I see. Was she close with any of the other actors?"

"Male actors?" Delila asks.

"Or female?" I say. Amelia would probably be more inclined to tell a female friend about the guy she was dating.

"Let's see. There was Anton. He moved away about two years ago. Went to New York City to audition for a few roles. I'd wager he's waiting tables right about now."

"Anyone else?" Mitchell asks, continuing to take notes.

"Oh, she was pretty close with Olivia Hill."

"Hill?" I ask. "Any relation to Theresa Hill at Hilltop House?"

"Yes, Theresa is her mother."

Theresa can't be a day over forty-five, and if Olivia was Amelia's age, that would mean Theresa had Olivia when she was still a teenager.

"I see you doing the math in your head," Delila says. "Let me help you out. Theresa got herself knocked up at sixteen. Had Olivia at seventeen. Her boyfriend at the time bailed on her. Wanted nothing to do with her or the baby. That's why Theresa never married."

"Do you happen to know the boyfriend's name?" Mitchell asks, and I can tell he's questioning if that's our killer. It feels wrong to me, though.

"Yeah, I went to school with them both. His name is Reggie Irving. He skipped town right after Theresa told him she was pregnant, and as far as I know, he's never come back."

If that's true, then Reggie has nothing to do with this. Still, I'll have Dad look into him. I shoot him a quick text, asking him to do just that.

"Any other friends of Amelia's that stick out in your memory?" Michell asks.

Delila sighs. "I'm afraid most have long since moved away. Even Olivia doesn't come around much anymore. Last I heard, she's married and living in Maryland. Gave up on the idea of acting years ago."

My phone vibrates in my hand, and I check my texts.

Dad: Reggie Irving died of an overdose when he was twenty-one.

Piper: Then he's definitely not our guy. Thanks, Dad.

I can't think of anything else to ask Delila. The theater turned out to be a big dead end. "Thank you for your time, Ms. Herschel," I say, using her preferred stage name.

Mitchell stands up and produces a card from his shirt pocket. "If you happen to think of anything else that might be helpful to the case, don't hesitate to call me."

She nods as she takes the card. "I'll see you out," she says.

We follow her to the back door. If so much time hadn't passed since Amelia's death, I would have wanted to see the stage, the dressing room, and anywhere Amelia might have been. But I'm sure Amelia's energy wouldn't be detectable anymore.

We walk back to the front of the building, noticing more cars in the lot. I watch as a few people, probably in their late teens and early twenties, talk in a group as they walk inside. They must be the latest crew of actors.

The second I'm inside the car, I call Dad. "So, Reggie Irving?" he says.

"Olivia Hill's biological father," I say. "Olivia was friends with Amelia, so we figured we'd look into her estranged father."

"There was no record of Reggie Irving having a daughter," Dad says.

"That's because he was a teenager when he got Theresa pregnant. He didn't want anything to do with a baby, so he left before Olivia was born and never looked back."

Dad makes a sound of disgust on the other end of the line. I know he doesn't understand how anyone could walk away from their child like that, but he's a great dad. I'm sure Mitchell doesn't have as difficult a time understanding Reggie's behavior since Mitchell's father wasn't much better after his wife died.

"What about Olivia Hill?" Dad asks, and I can hear his fingers clicking away on his laptop.

"According to the theater owner, Olivia lives in Maryland now."

"I'll look into her and give her a call," Dad says. "Her number is probably listed, and we could find out if she knew of anyone who was stalking Amelia."

"Except this guy wasn't stalking her. I'm sure of it. It was someone she knew. Someone she went to for help." I rub my forehead. If Amelia was close to this guy, why can't I see him in my visions? Probably because I'm reading a damn bird cage. "That's it!"

"What's it?" both Dad and Mitchell ask.

"I need something else of Amelia's to read. The killer knew Amelia, talked to her on the phone, but he was never inside her apartment."

"What makes you say that?" Mitchell says.

"The bird would have seen him."

"Unless the cage was covered," Dad says.

"Implying this guy was only ever with Amelia at night."

Chills run through me at Mitchell's words. "She was seeing him."

"You mean he was her boyfriend?" Mitchell asks.

"I don't know for sure. I'm sensing something off about the relationship."

Mitchell still hasn't started the car, probably because we don't have our next move figured out. He taps the steering wheel as he thinks. "Well, he did wind up killing her, so that sounds about right."

"No. It's more than that. I don't think we're going to find anyone who can name this guy."

"Pumpkin, someone had to know who he was," Dad says through the speakerphone.

"Who he was, yes, but maybe not that he was connected to Amelia." I'm missing something. Something just outside my senses. "Play the game," I say, adding, "Dad."

Mitchell stiffens beside me. He knows I still don't forgive him for taking advantage of the game earlier.

"Dad, the game," I insist. "I need to know why no one can name this guy."

"What did you eat for breakfast?" he begins.

"Crumb cake."

"Where's Jezebel?"

"With Mom and Max."

"What was Amelia's best friend's name?"

"Olivia Hill."

"How did Amelia know her killer?"

"She was sleeping with him."

"Who knew about their relationship?"

"No one." My eyes open. "Their relationship was a secret."

CHAPTER SEVENTEEN

Usually, finding out the victim knew their killer is good news because it gives me a list of suspects. But the fact that their relationship was a secret just made this case all that much more difficult.

"It could be anyone, literally anyone in her life. Her uncle's friends even," I say.

"Her uncle isn't much older than Amelia was, so that's true," Mitchell says. "And if she was dating one of her uncle's friends, I don't think he'd be too happy about it, which means they'd keep it a secret."

"Good thinking, Mitchell," Dad says. "Why don't you and Piper pay Jacob Crane another visit. Get a list of his friends to look into. I'll call Olivia. Maybe Amelia did confide in someone, or even if she didn't, it's possible Olivia had her suspicions considering she and Amelia were close."

"Thanks, Dad. Keep us posted, and we'll do the same," I say, ending the call.

Mitchell clicks his seat belt. "What are the odds Jacob Crane is home at this hour on a Friday?"

"Not good since his wife told us he works until six." I search on my phone, trying to locate Jacob Crane's psychology practice. "Got it. His office is on Third Street." I set the GPS, and Mitchell gets us there in fifteen minutes.

The office building looks like an old church. The front door is a huge, wooden archway. Mitchell opens it, and we step inside. It's dark. Like really dark. The only lighting is coming from sconces on the walls.

"I feel like we just stepped back in time," Mitchell whispers to me as we approach a brunette woman in her early twenties at a receptionist desk.

"Hello," I say. "We're looking for Jacob Crane. Is he in?"

"Dr. Crane just finished with a client. Let me see if he's accepting visitors." She picks up her desk phone. "Your names?"

"Piper Ashwell and Detective Brennan. We spoke to Dr. Crane just the other day," I add in case he's already forgotten our names.

"Dr. Crane, there's a Pepper Ashwell and Detective Brenaman here to see you."

Mitchell and I exchange a look at how she butchered both our names. Truth be told, it's probably good she got our names incorrect since I accused Jacob and his wife of trying to kill Amelia the last time we saw them.

"Yes, sir. I'll send them back." She hangs up and smiles at us. "You're in luck. Dr. Crane has an opening and can see you." She points a finger over her shoulder. "You'll want to head to the stairwell and go up to the second floor. Dr. Crane's office is the second door on the right."

"Thank you," I say.

"After you, *Pepper*," Mitchell says with a smile.

"You're too kind, *Brenaman*," I reply.

The receptionist was wrong about the location of Jacob's office. The second door on the right is a supply closet. I roll my eyes as I knock on the second door on the left instead. To my surprise, Rebecca Crane answers the door.

"Can I help you?" she asks, giving us a very annoyed look. "I'm in the middle of a session with a client."

"I thought you worked from home," I say.

"Usually I do, but I do have some clients who see me in person every so often to help them get over their issues with leaving the house." She pulls the door shut behind her, most likely in an attempt to keep the identity of her client a secret. "But I'm not sure why I'm telling either of you anything after the heinous accusations you made in my own home."

Since I no longer believe they actually did harm Amelia, though only because Amelia moved out before they could put their sick plan into motion, I decide to play nice. We need information after all. "New information in the case has cleared you and your husband."

"Well, I should think so. I'm not sure how you came up with that crazy idea in the first place."

The only crazy thing here is her. "We do need to speak with your husband, though," I say. "The receptionist gave us the wrong directions to his office."

Rebecca rolls her eyes. "That woman is a moron. I swear. I told Jacob we shouldn't have hired her. Anyone else would have been better. A monkey would have been better."

"I'd go to a psychologist who had a monkey for a receptionist," Mitchell says beside me.

I jab my elbow into his stomach. "Dr. Crane, could you please tell us where we can find your husband? We don't want to keep you from your client any longer."

"Third floor, third door on the left," she says before ducking back inside her office.

"She's so pleasant," I say as we head upstairs.

"Yeah, she's pleasant, the receptionist is a genius, and this building isn't creepy in the least. I could stay here all day." Mitchell follows me to the third door on the left. "It's a wonder the actual clients don't get lost and wind up in the offices of the wrong psychologists."

I knock on the door, but not before I hear Jacob talking on the phone. I have no doubt Rebecca called to tell him I no longer think they had anything to do with Amelia's death.

Jacob Crane answers. "Detectives, come in." He steps aside so we can enter. Unlike the rest of this building, Jacob's office has good lighting, though it's due to the large window taking up most of the side wall. "I didn't think I'd be hearing from you both again so soon. Did you discover anything else concerning my niece's murder?" He sits down at his desk instead of the armchair, which makes me happy because I wasn't about to sit on that couch like I was one of his patients. I could only imagine the field day a psychologist would have analyzing me. Or Mitchell for that matter.

Mitchell looks just as relieved as I am to be in a regular chair. "Dr. Crane, we recently were made aware of the fact that Amelia was engaged in a secret relationship."

Jacob shakes his head. "I wasn't aware of that."

Hence, it was a secret. I stop myself from rolling my eyes. "Yes, well we also believe it was a secret for a reason. Like perhaps it was one of your friends who knew you'd be upset if you discovered he was dating your niece."

He sits forward and leans his elbows on the desk. "One of my friends?" He laughs and jerks back in his chair. "That's preposterous. My friends knew better. Sure, Amelia wasn't much younger than we were at the time, but she was off-limits. I would have—" He stops short and clears his throat.

"You would have what?" Mitchell asks.

Jacob adjusts his red and white striped tie. "I would have put an end to the relationship immediately."

"Do you think there's any possibility that your niece moved out because she didn't want you to discover the relationship?" I ask.

He shakes his head. "No. No way. None of my friends would do that to me."

"We understand you feel that way, but we'd still like a list of friends you had at the time Amelia moved out of your house," Mitchell says.

"Only the ones who lived within two hours of here," I add. I don't need a list of his social media contacts all over the planet.

"I assure you there was nothing going on between Amelia and any of my friends."

"And you're probably correct," I say, although I'm not convinced of it at all. I'm just sensing the doctor is about to lose his mind—ironically enough. "I can easily put an end to this assumption if you'll just write me a list of names."

"I'm not following," he says.

"I have a special knack for looking at lists and seeing more to a person's name." I don't want to flat out tell him I'm psychic because then he'll know exactly how I discovered his sick plan to drug Amelia and steal her inheritance. I'm still angry that he and Rebecca wound up with the money in the end anyway.

"I'm not a fan of your methods at all. You make accusations with absolutely nothing to back them up."

He's right about one thing. I shouldn't have blurted out what I read off the photo in his house. I should have told Dad and Mitchell and devised a plan to catch Rebecca and Jacob somehow.

"You do want to find the person responsible for killing your niece, don't you?" I ask. "Because I can assure you that while Levi O'Neil played his role in Amelia's murder, he's not the one who actually strangled her."

"She was strangled?" he asks, and for the first time, I see some hint of emotion for his niece.

Mitchell nods. "You were notified when her body was recovered."

"Yes, but the officer I spoke to didn't tell me how she died."

And I can imagine the state of Amelia's body when it was recovered. I doubt Jacob even when down to the morgue to ID her.

He pinches the bridge of his nose and starts to cry.

Mitchell and I exchange a look. This isn't the same man we met before. I make a snap decision and reach for his hand, pretending to console him in his moment of weakness.

"I can't go down there. It was one thing to tell her she was sick and give her sugar pills. But to see her dead body..." Jacob breaks down.

Rebecca moves toward the desk. "I'll tell them you're too distraught. They can ID her from her DNA."

I let go of Jacob's hand. "Dr. Crane, I know you didn't want Amelia to die, and I apologize for suggesting you were behind this. But you should know that I'm a psychic

P.I., and I read the energy off that photograph in your house. I saw the plan you concocted to have one of your colleagues falsely diagnose Amelia so you could get control of her money. And just now, I saw that you did mourn your niece's death. You might not have been the model uncle, but you certainly didn't want her dead."

"You're psychic?" he asks, widening his eyes at me.

"Yes. So, you can see why I reacted the way I did at your home."

"I'd never hurt her. I needed the money at the time. My practice had no clients. We were going to lose everything, and Amelia had so much money she didn't know what to do with. She moved out before I did anything. I kept stalling. Rebecca asked me about it. Asked when I was sending Amelia to see Steven."

"Steven who?" Mitchell asks.

"Steven Moore. He worked here for the first two years the practice was open."

"He's not here anymore?" I ask.

Jacob shakes his head. "He left before Amelia died."

Before Jacob and Rebecca got all of Amelia's money.

Mitchell jots down the name. "What about that list of your friends?" Mitchell asks. "Piper here can simply look at the list and know if someone was involved in your niece's murder."

Jacob looks a little disbelieving at that, but he picks up his pen and writes a list of names on his legal pad. Then he tears off the top sheet and slides it across the desk to me.

"These were my closest friends at the time. The ones I hung out with, at least."

"Did they come by your house as well?" Mitchell asks, and I know he's trying to figure out if these men would have had a way to meet Amelia before she moved out.

"We had a weekly poker game," Jacob says. "Amelia mostly avoided us, but they all knew her if that's what you're asking."

"Did any of them show interest in her?" Mitchell asks.

I allow myself to look at the list of names. "Jax Dawson," I say.

"Yeah," Jacob says. "He made a comment about Amelia's shorts being so short. I put an end to it immediately, though. I told them all that she was off-limits. No one ever said another thing. Jax used to work here as well. He was smart enough not to jeopardize his career by making any more comments about my niece."

Mitchell is eyeing me, trying to figure out if I'm getting anything more from Jax's name. I'm not. I never know why names jump out at me. It could be that Mitchell asked the right question and my senses answered. Or there could be more to it. I give him a slight nod, letting him know we should look into Jax Dawson.

One of my other visions of Rebecca and Jacob comes to mind. The one where Rebecca called Jacob and told him we were stopping by the house to ask them a few questions. Jacob said he didn't want to rehash the case because it had been hard enough the first time. "Thank you for your time, Dr. Crane. And we're sorry to make you go through this again. I'm sure Amelia's death was difficult for you."

"Thank you," he says.

"We'll see ourselves out," Mitchell tells him.

I take the list of names, and we leave Jacob to his emotions.

"Do you believe him?" Mitchell asks once we're in the stairwell.

"I do. I think he thought his plan to fake her diagnosis was harmless because he wouldn't actually be drugging her. He needed money to get his business off the ground, but he never wanted Amelia to die. And when she did and he got her money, I think he felt so guilty about ever concocting that plan."

"What about Rebecca?" Mitchell asks. "She seems so unfeeling. Cold."

She does. "I didn't pick up on any remorse from her, just relief when I told her we didn't suspect her or Jacob anymore."

"So where to next? Do we check out Jax Dawson?" Mitchell asks.

"You got it."

We say goodbye to the receptionist, who looks at us like she's never seen us before in her life.

"If Jacob and Rebecca had followed through with their plan to drug Rebecca, I'd suspect they were also slipping their receptionist some pills," Mitchell says as we step outside.

"More like she's sneaking pills from empty offices," I say.

"Fact?" Mitchell asks me.

"I'm guessing, but I get the feeling I'm right."

"I might need to follow up on that later," Mitchell says.

"Knock your socks off, Detective, but first, let's go talk to Jax Dawson."

Mitchell finds the address for Jax's current place of employment, which is actually at the hospital. I call Dad on the way and fill him in.

"Well, that's more interesting than you realize," Dad says through the speaker phone when I tell him where we're heading.

"Why is that?" I ask, giving Mitchell a sideways glance.

"Because the only tip Olivia had for me when I asked if Amelia ever mentioned any of her uncle's friends hitting on her was that one in particular liked to make inappropriate comments."

"Jax Dawson," Mitchell says. "So much for Jacob thinking he'd put an end to it."

"So they could have been secretly dating," I say.

"I don't think so," Dad says.

"Which one of us is the psychic here?" I joke.

"You, pumpkin, but you're missing a key piece of information."

"What's that?" Mitchell asks.

"According to Olivia, Amelia was convinced Jax Dawson was having an affair with Rebecca Crane."

CHAPTER EIGHTEEN

So many truths slam into my mind all at once I have to press my fingers to both temples in an attempt to keep my head from exploding.

"Piper?" Mitchell asks, turning on the siren and lights and immediately pulling across traffic to park on the shoulder of the road.

"What's going on over there?" Dad asks through the phone, which is now in my lap since I dropped it.

"Shh!" I say. I need quiet. It's so loud inside my head right now.

Mitchell takes my head in his hands and gently turns my face toward him. He removes my fingers from my face and starts massaging my temples with the pads of his thumbs. I stare at him, and my mind quiets.

"Rebecca is only with Jacob because of the money. She's still seeing Jax. That's the real reason why he left the practice. They didn't think they could keep the affair going under Jacob's nose like that. Jax wasn't even commenting on Amelia's shorts that day during the poker game. He was commenting on Rebecca's, but Amelia happened to be walking by, and Jacob assumed that's who Jax was talking about."

Mitchell smiles at me. "You got all that? Just now?"

"At a price. My head is about to explode."

"Mitchell, take her back to your condo. I'll talk to Dawson."

"No," I say. "We don't know if he's dangerous. If he was working with Rebecca to get Amelia's money..." I cringe as my head throbs.

"Mr. Ashwell, wait for us. I'll take Piper to my place and get her a cold pack and some aspirin. We'll meet up at the hospital around five to talk to Dawson together."

"Thanks, Mitchell," Dad says. "And it's Thomas or Tom. Cut the Mr. Ashwell crap."

Mitchell laughs. "Can't do it, sir." He disconnects the call and places my phone in the middle console. "What am I going to do with you, Piper?" He continues to massage my temples, his face inches from mine.

"Aspirin," I say. Normally, I avoid aspirin because it affects my ability to have visions, but right now I need Mitchell to stop being so sweet to me.

He leans toward me, and I tense, not sure what he's going to do. He places a kiss on my forehead, and when he pulls away, he looks completely embarrassed. "I'm sorry."

He clears his throat and starts the engine. Without another word, he pulls back onto the road and drives us to his condo.

I wake up nearly four hours later. Thankfully, my head feels normal after the aspirin. I remove the cold pack, which is no longer cold, from my forehead and stare up at the ceiling in Mitchell's room. I don't want him to know I'm awake yet. I need time to think about what happened in the car. Lately, it's taking more effort to push Mitchell away than to let him in. But I'm not sure either one of us is ready for this. He looked so completely embarrassed when he kissed my forehead, and I can't help wondering if he's never done that before. I think these emotions might be as new for him as they are for me.

God, we're both completely hopeless.

I count to fifty before working up enough resolve to face him. I walk out into the living room, where he's watching TV. He immediately turns it off when I enter the room.

"Hey, how are you feeling?"

"Much better. Thanks for taking care of me."

"Of course." He pats the couch next to him. "Want to sit?"

No. Too much. Too soon. "Shouldn't we get going? We told my dad we'd meet him at the hospital at five."

"Right." Mitchell stands up. "Let me get the bird some more water." He disappears into the kitchen, and I move toward the bird.

"Hi, Jeffrey."

Jeffrey whistles in response.

"Isn't it weird that Hugo Spencer's bird talked, but Jeffrey just seems to whistle?" I ask when Mitchell returns with the water.

"Maybe Amelia liked to whistle. Pets tend to imitate their owners. Not just birds, either. Jez can give me that judgmental look you throw my way all the time," he jokes.

I roll my eyes. "That's because she's smart and you deserve it most of the time, but you're probably right about Jeffrey," I say.

The hospital is eighteen minutes away, but since we're behind schedule and we are on official police business, Mitchell throws on the lights, minus the siren, and gets us there in fourteen and a half minutes.

"I'm telling my dad you were speeding with his daughter in the car," I say as we enter the hospital.

"Please don't. He still hasn't forgiven me for the accident I got us into." He holds the door open for me.

"Well, that was entirely your fault for being jealous that I talked to another man." I pat the front of his shirt, and we both look down at my hand. Dear Lord, why am I touching his chest?

Dad picks that exact moment to show up.

I quickly lower my hand and tuck my hair behind my

ear. “Any idea where Dawson’s office would be located?” I ask, quickly changing the subject.

“Yeah, follow me,” Dad says, his gaze volleying between Mitchell and me. Dad brings us to a set of elevators, and we take one up to the sixth floor. There’s an office to the left when we step off the elevator. “Here.”

The frosted glass door is only partially see-through, but it’s clear someone’s inside. Mitchell raises his hand and knocks with two knuckles. “Dr. Dawson?” he calls.

I see the form on the other side get up and approach the door.

“Can I help you?” Dawson asks once he opens the door, his eyes taking in Mitchell first and then me.

Mitchell flashes his badge. “Detective Brennan. These are my partners, Piper Ashwell and Thomas Ashwell. We’d like to ask you a few questions about Amelia Crane.”

“Amelia?” Dawson shakes his head. “Didn’t she die a few years ago?”

Playing dumb is never a good idea, but doing it with a psychic is just plain stupid. Not that he knows I’m psychic. “Yes, but your affair with her aunt is still going strong,” I say.

Dawson looks around the hallway, probably trying to figure out if anyone overheard me. “Come inside.” He ushers us in and closes the door.

“Tell me what you think you know,” Dawson begins as he retakes his seat.

"Actually, we're going to ask the questions," Mitchell says.

"Or, I could pick up that pen on your desk and read the energy off it to find out what we need to know." I bob my shoulders. "Either way. Oh, silly me. I forgot to mention I'm a psychometrist. A psychic if you're more familiar with that term."

"What is this about exactly?" Dawson asks.

Dad's positioned himself by the door, possibly to block Dawson's exit while Mitchell and I question him.

Mitchell takes a seat and whips out his pad and pen. "We've recently spoken with Jacob and Rebecca Crane. Your name came up."

"Yes, you see, Jacob was under the impression that you might have had an impure thought or two about his niece Amelia, but I don't think that's true," I say, sitting beside Mitchell. "I think you've been having an affair with Jacob's wife for some time now. That's why you left Jacob's practice, isn't it?"

"You expect me to believe Jacob told you this?" he asks with a smirk.

"No. He didn't. He has no clue that you and Rebecca are running around behind his back. But we know." I make a circular motion with my finger, indicating Mitchell, Dad, and me. "And we can keep this quiet if you're willing to answer our questions. But if you're uncooperative, then we'll have to go back and have another chat with Jacob and Rebecca, one that will include your name quite a bit."

"Is this legal?" Dawson asks Mitchell.

"I'm sorry, but I zoned out for a minute there. Did Piper start asking you questions already?" Mitchell even goes so far as to look to Dad for a response as well.

I can't help smiling at Mitchell. The man really does have my back in every way possible. He's seriously going to be the death of me, though, because he's making me rethink my entire life outside of my job. Worse, the expression on Dad's face says he's well aware of what I'm thinking.

"Piper?" Mitchell prods.

"Right. So, how long has the affair been going on?"

Dawson huffs. "If I talk, do you swear this stays between us?"

"Like I said, I don't even need you to talk. I can find out what I need to know on my own, but I don't think either of us wants me to do that." I really don't want to. What other people do behind closed doors is none of my business. I don't want to see it.

"About ten years."

Ten years. Longer than I thought. "How did you keep it from Jacob?"

"I talked about other women, so he never suspected. Then, at a poker game one night, I made that comment about Rebecca's shorts. I didn't even realize I said that out loud. I screwed up, and it could have ruined everything. I got lucky when Amelia walked by at that exact moment and Jacob thought I was referring to her."

"Did you leave the firm, or did he push you out?" Mitchell asks.

"I left at Rebecca's request. She said it was too hard to conceal her feelings for me with her husband in the same building."

Gag. Dawson is an attractive man, but I don't understand how anyone could possibly juggle two men at once. I can't handle one.

"Did you know Amelia had a boyfriend before she died?" I ask.

He shakes his head. "Rebecca never mentioned it."

"You never saw Amelia with anyone?"

"Once. I was with Rebecca, and we almost ran into Amelia. She was in the same movie theater as us."

"Are you saying you and Rebecca went on actual dates?" Dad asks.

"Not as much anymore," Dawson says. "We're more careful now after we almost got caught. You see, Jacob hates the movies, and since they're dark, we figured it was a good place for us to go without being caught. When we weren't at my place, anyway."

"Who was Amelia with?" I ask, not wanting details about Dawson and Rebecca.

"I don't know. I'd never seen the guy, and like I said, it was dark. He was wearing a baseball cap, so his face was in shadow. And he was seated. Amelia got up to use the restroom right when Rebecca and I walked in. We were able to dodge her, thankfully, and I kept an eye out for her after that."

"Why didn't you leave the theater? Why would you risk getting caught?" I ask.

"Rebecca liked the thrill of it. She said it turned her on."

God, this conversation is getting more uncomfortable every minute. Mitchell must sense my unease because he picks up with the line of questioning. "Anything else you noticed about the man? Age? Height? Weight?"

"Not really. He was sitting, but I suppose he was pretty tall judging by the fact that no one sat behind him. No one likes to sit behind tall people in the movie theater, right?" He gives a nervous chuckle. "You swear you won't tell Jacob any of this?" he asks.

"You have our word," I say, standing up.

Mitchell follows my lead, and we start for the door, which Dad opens for us.

"Oh, wait. There was one more thing," Dawson says. "In the movie, the lead actress was undressing, and someone in the audience whistled really loudly. I turned around and saw Amelia smacking her date."

"He was the one who whistled," I say, my senses tingling.

"Yeah, not that it's really important, but he did it three more times before the movie was over, so I remembered it."

Actually, it's really important. "Thank you," I say, stepping out into the hallway.

"What's that look for?" Mitchell asks me.

"I was on to something in your condo when I asked about why Jeffrey whistles. He does it because Amelia's late-night boyfriend did it."

"You're sure he's our killer?"

"He's our killer all right."

CHAPTER NINETEEN

We don't discuss the case until we're in the parking lot, standing next to Mitchell's patrol car.

"We should go talk to Rebecca," I say. "It's possible she was able to recognize something about our whistler that Dawson couldn't."

"Rebecca is probably home by now," Dad says.

That's true. I check my watch. "But Jacob will be home soon as well."

"Do we really go there and out the affair?" Mitchell asks. "I mean I'm not a fan of either of them, but is it really our call to mess up a marriage?"

"It's our job to solve this case, but I have an idea. Let's go see Jacob first."

Dad crosses his arms. "What are you up to, pumpkin?"

"You'll see," I say, opening the passenger door. "Meet

you there. It's the building that looks like a church on Third Street. You can't miss it."

Once we're on the road, Mitchell says, "What's the plan?"

"Dawson said he and Rebecca have been sneaking around for about ten years now. How would Jacob have no idea that's going on? I mean the three of them worked together at one point."

"And Dawson did slip up at that poker game. If it happened once, odds are it happened again." Mitchell tightens his grip on the steering wheel. "But if Jacob does know about the affair, why would he stay with Rebecca? I mean he could have had all of Amelia's money for himself."

"Not necessarily. Divorcing her would most likely give her half of everything he has."

Mitchell nods. "You're right. So, he chooses to stay with her to keep her from getting a bigger cut of the money." Something is clearly still bothering him judging by how tense he is.

"You hate cheaters," I say.

He nods again. "I just don't understand cheating. If you don't want to be with someone, break up. Don't start seeing someone else. It's just..." He shakes his head.

"You've never cheated on anyone," I say. "Good to know."

He eyes me for a brief moment. "I've never technically

been in a relationship, so it's kind of hard to cheat. But I wouldn't. Not ever."

"I wouldn't either. To be honest, the thought of juggling two men is not in the least bit appealing to me."

Mitchell laughs. "I could have guessed that."

"I have to wonder why Rebecca didn't file for divorce, though. If she'd really get half of Jacob's money, I'd think she'd be all for that. She gets the man she wants and the money she wants. It's a win-win."

Mitchell snaps his fingers. "Unless there was a prenup involved that said if either cheated, they'd get nothing."

"But then why wouldn't Jacob have left her and kept all the money for himself?" I ask. This case is getting stranger by the minute.

"I guess that's a question we need to ask him."

The receptionist is gone for the day, so Mitchell and I bring Dad right up to Jacob's office. His door is open, but Mitchell knocks anyway.

"Detectives, what are you doing back here?" Jacob asks.

I step around Mitchell, determined to put everything out in the open and witness Jacob's response for myself. "Dr. Crane, I'm afraid we have some upsetting news for you. Is your wife gone for the day?"

"Yes, she left about two hours ago. Why?" He gestures to the couch, possibly sensing this conversation is going to be a doozy.

I sit down sandwiched between Dad and Mitchell.

"Dr. Crane, I don't like to get involved in people's personal lives, but this case has uncovered some details that I need to bring to your attention."

"Oh. This is about Rebecca and Jax."

Dad, Mitchell, and I probably all look like we were sucker punched.

"You think I don't know?" Jacob wipes a tear from his left eye. "I knew soon after it started. At first, I just thought it was Jax being Jax. He loves women. All women."

I can't help looking at Mitchell, and I immediately regret doing so because his face falls. I know he's not like that anymore, and I just made him think I still view him that way. He probably thinks all the talks we've had were for nothing. I subtly slide my leg toward his so our knees are touching. Okay, so I suck at consoling people or showing emotion at all, but what else am I supposed to do with Dad and Jacob sitting right here?

"If you know, why do you stay with your wife?" Dad asks.

Jacob looks completely distraught. "I love my wife. If I confronted her, I would have lost her. I had no money back then. My practice wasn't even off the ground yet. If I lost her, I would have lost everything. She's my world."

Realization dawns on me as the pieces fall into place. There is no Steven Moore. Jacob made up that name to throw us off. It was Jax all along. "Dawson was the colleague you were going to have falsely diagnose Amelia. You were trying to set him up."

Jacob nods. "If Jax was in prison, Rebecca would have to stop seeing him, and Amelia wasn't going to get hurt either. I was going to make sure of it."

"By switching the pills Dawson prescribed for sugar pills," I say.

"I know I wasn't a good uncle, but I did love my niece. I tried to give her some freedom. And the money I wanted from her, I was going to give it back once I got on my feet. I swear. I've done some questionable things, but I'm not a murderer."

That doesn't matter anymore. Amelia would never know it, and there's no way to prove something that never happened.

"After Amelia died, I thought the money would make Rebecca end things with Jax. I mean how in love with him could she really be?" Jacob starts to cry. "I keep telling myself she has to love us both or she wouldn't stay." He meets my gaze. "That has to be it, right? Otherwise, she'd divorce me and take half the money."

He's asking me for relationship insight? Oh boy. "Dr. Crane, I did read your wife once, and I got the sense she didn't want to go through the emotional turmoil of reopening Amelia's case. But I also sense she doesn't like to deal with emotional issues at all outside of her work." Seeing as Jacob has cried in front of me numerous times, I'm willing to bet Rebecca tries to avoid his emotional outbursts as well. "I think she has a hard time dealing with your emotions, and divorcing you would cause you to be emotional."

"You're saying she's staying with me to avoid making me cry?" He wipes his cheeks with the backs of his hands.

"I'd like to weigh in here," Mitchell says, raising a hand as if he were in school. "I think she knows you're aware of the affair. Right now, she has everything she wants. Jax, money, and you. If she divorces you, she'd have to go out on her own as far as the practice is concerned. It's more work than she wants to get into."

"Very insightful, Mitchell," I whisper. "Dr. Crane, I'm sensing what Detective Brennan is saying is in fact true."

"Why are you all here?" Jacob asks. "It couldn't just be to tell me about Rebecca."

"No, it's not," I say. "Jax told us he and Rebecca ran into Amelia at the movie theater with her boyfriend one night. We're convinced it was Amelia's boyfriend who murdered her, but the problem is, no one seems to know who he was."

"And you think Rebecca knows?" Jacob shakes his head. "She would have told me."

He's right. She would have helped solve the case if for no other reason than to give Jacob closure so he'd stop crying. "I don't think she got a good look at him, but if she was able to make out any of his features, it might help us narrow down who the man is."

"You think he's still living in town?" Jacob asks, his voice cracking.

"He got away with murder. Why wouldn't he be?"

"You can't tell Rebecca I know about the affair. Please." He actually presses his palms together in front of him.

"Call your wife," Dad says. "Tell her you have to work late. We'll go talk to her now before you go home."

I'm more than a little surprised Dad is willing to keep this secret. He and Mom have been happily married for thirty years. And Dad feels the same way about cheaters as Mitchell does. But I suppose Jacob is the victim in this situation, and Dad must feel for him.

"Thank you. I'll do that right now. I can't tell you how much this means to me," Jacob stands up when we do and shakes all our hands.

"I'm tired of you screwing up, Jax. I want you gone," Jacob says, his face bright red.

"The prescriptions are close enough that no one will be any the wiser. I'll meet with Mrs. Orsen in a few days and tell her I found something that might be more effective. I'll write a new prescription. No harm done."

Jacob rips his hand from mine. "What did you do?" he asks me.

"It was what you did," I say. "I try not to shake people's hands because some people are harder not to read than to read."

"What did you see?" he asks me, still looking a little too terrified for someone who hasn't done anything wrong.

"You were yelling at Jax for giving a patient the wrong prescription. Jax told us he left this office at Rebecca's request, but I'm sensing that's not true."

"It is in part," Jacob says. "I told Rebecca what Jax did."

"Because you thought it would make her stop seeing him," I say, knowing it's true.

"I was grasping at straws. She told him it would be better if he found a different practice."

That's not the story Jax told, but I don't want to see Jacob cry again, so I don't tell him that.

"Thank you for your help, Dr. Crane," I say.

"Well, that was interesting," Mitchell says as we walk out to our cars. "I still don't see how you can love a person who is cheating on you."

"I agree with you there," Dad says.

"Jacob clearly isn't okay with the cheating. He was so angry in the vision I just had, and I don't think the anger had much to do with Jax's screwup with the prescriptions."

"Let's go see Rebecca before Jacob goes home," Dad says. "I'll meet you two there."

Mitchell is quiet on the drive, and I can practically see the little hamster running on its wheel inside his head.

"What are you thinking?" I finally ask.

"Is this another reason why you avoid relationships?

Because seeing things like the Rebecca, Jacob, and Jax love triangle turns your stomach?"

"I'd never be in a situation like they are because no one could keep a secret like that from me." I twist the ring on my pinky finger. "Even thoughts about another person would surface, and I'm not sure that's entirely fair because a person can have thoughts and not act on them."

"Are you saying you know whenever I find a woman attractive?" Mitchell asks, and for once there is no trace of sarcasm or confidence in his tone.

"Finding someone attractive doesn't necessarily mean you're attracted to them," I say.

"True." He clears his voice. "Were you attracted to Ryker—I mean Sam?"

Sam Pierce is a special circumstance. "I found him attractive on the outside. And I was attracted to what he could do as a psychic. But once I found out he was a kidnapper, I was completely repulsed by him."

"What about me?" Mitchell asks, keeping his gaze on the road.

"Could we not have this conversation right now?"

"Is there a conversation to have?" This time he looks at me.

I can't keep dodging this. It's only making things more complicated between us. "I know I don't want to talk about it. I'd rather just..." I don't know how to say it.

"See where things go?" Mitchell asks.

"Yeah." I stop playing with my ring and slide my hands under my legs.

"Okay. I can respect that."

"Thanks." I stare out the window until we're in the Crane's driveway.

Dad looks suspiciously between Mitchell and me as we walk up to the front door, but he doesn't question us. I'm grateful for that much. Mitchell rings the bell, and Rebecca Crane couldn't look unhappier when she greets us.

"Again?" she asks. "I thought you said you didn't think my husband and I had anything to do with Amelia's murder."

"We don't," I say. "But we had an interesting conversation with Jax Dawson, and we'd like to ask you a few questions about the man you two saw with Amelia at the movie theater." I decide laying it all out there is the best way to get our foot in the door.

"Luckily for you, Jacob is working late this evening." She steps aside. "Come in."

I give Dad a small smile as we enter the house.

"Please don't make yourselves too comfortable. I don't know exactly how long it will be before Jacob comes home, and I'd rather you be gone when he does."

"We just have one question, so this won't take long," I say, remaining in the entryway.

"Wonderful." Her tone implies it's anything but.

"Mr. Dawson already gave us his description of the man Amelia was with. We'd just like to get yours."

"That's it?" she asks.

"That's it." I shrug like it's no big deal.

She lets out a deep breath and looks up at the ceiling as if the memory is stored up there. "Okay, well, it was dark, so I didn't get a good look at him. He was pretty tall. Average build, but he was wearing a jacket, so I can't be sure if I was mostly seeing jacket or if he was filling it out. He had on a baseball cap, so I didn't see his face. And he kept whistling during the movie." She lowers her head to look at us again. "That's all I've got."

"You never saw her with anyone that could have fit the man's description after that night?" I ask.

"No. Now if you'll please leave. I've told you all I could." She opens the front door.

"Wait. I have one more question," Mitchell says. "I've got to know why you're staying with Jacob. Why continue to juggle two men when you don't have to?"

She takes a step toward Mitchell. "Detective, my husband worships me. He gives me everything I could ever want and treats me like a queen. Jax fulfills other needs that I won't get into with you. Does that answer your question?"

"Thank you for your time," I say, pushing Mitchell out the door.

"I think it's time we call it a night," Dad says. "The

funeral for Hugo Spencer is tomorrow. See you both there?"

"Yeah, see you there. Oh, and give Jez a kiss for me. I really miss her."

"She misses you just as much, pumpkin." Dad kisses my cheek before getting into his BMW.

"Ready to go home?" Mitchell asks me once we're in the patrol car.

"I'd love to, but I'm stuck at your place for the time being."

"Don't sound so put out. I'm the one sleeping on the couch."

"Sorry for intruding on your personal space like this."

"You're not intruding. Besides, you let me crash at your place all the time."

"Where you sleep on the couch," I say with a laugh. "You can't win."

"I beg to differ."

I do my best not to read into the meaning of his words.

I wake up Saturday morning to something brushing against my face. I raise my hand to swat away whatever is tickling me.

Amelia throws her arms around the man's waist. "I'm scared. He's everywhere. I don't know what to do anymore.

I know you don't want me going to the police, but what if I hire a private investigator? I have plenty of money."

Firm hands grip her arms and push her away. "To do what? You know he's following you. A P.I. isn't going to do anything but take your money. I'll handle it."

"But it's been going on for months. I can't keep living this way. I have to do something. I'm sorry if you don't agree, but this is my life." Amelia turns away.

A hand grabs her and spins her back around. "Don't you walk away from me. I said I've got this." He loosens his grip, and his tone softens. "Come on, baby. Let me take you away from here. Just the two of us. That guy will never find you again, and we have plenty of money between us to live long, happy lives." He leans forward and kisses her, but she pushes against his chest.

"No. I don't want to leave. This is my home. I tried it your way. Now I'm doing it my way."

"I'm afraid that's not an option, love." He reaches for her neck and squeezes.

CHAPTER TWENTY

"Piper!" Mitchell rushes into the room and shoos the bird off me. "What happened?"

I'm choking and grabbing at the invisible hands squeezing my neck.

Mitchell sits me up and removes my hands so he can examine my neck. "Nothing's there. I'm assuming this is the effect of a vision."

I still can't talk, so I nod.

"I'm never going to get used to seeing you like this after a vision." He sits next to me in the bed and wraps one arm around my shoulders. I try not to overthink it as I lay my head on his chest. "God, Piper, loving you is the hardest damn thing I've ever done."

I jerk my head up, suddenly not aware of the phantom pain in my neck. I meet his gaze.

"I didn't mean to say that out loud," he says. "I take it back."

We stare at each other, both at a loss for words. No one other than my parents has ever said they love me, and I don't know what to do with this information.

Finally, he says, "Tell me about the vision."

I swallow hard, thankful to focus on the case and not Mitchell's feelings for me. "I saw the killer strangle Amelia."

"Did you see who it was?"

I lower my gaze. "The vision was from Jeffery's perspective, and he was definitely positioned behind the murderer. I don't think this guy intended to kill her. He just reacted in a heated moment."

"Do you think he was after her money then?" Mitchell asks.

"Yeah. I think he hired O'Neil to scare her so that he could then convince her to run away with him. And take the money with them, of course. But she refused to leave and said if he didn't want her to go to the police, then she'd go to a private investigator instead."

"He probably didn't want her spending any of the money he planned to get his hands on," Mitchell says.

"And I think he was trying to protect O'Neil by not letting Amelia go to the authorities. A P.I. would have told her to report him."

"The question remains, how do we find this guy?"

"I wish I knew."

Mitchell gets up from the bed. "I should go catch Jeffrey and get him back in the cage before we head to the funeral this morning."

"How did he get out anyway?" I ask, getting out of the bed myself.

"I must not have latched his cage properly last night when I fed him."

I can't say I'm all that upset considering I now know how Amelia died. "He must have killed her late at night while they were in her apartment."

"But if Jeffrey witnessed it, it couldn't have been late at night," Mitchell says. "His cage is covered at night."

"I have a feeling the people who donated her things had to put Jeffrey back in his cage before sending him to Hilltop House."

"You think he got out just like he did last night."

"Seems to make sense, and in my vision, Jeffrey's view of the killer was partially obstructed, like he was perched on a shelf with either a picture frame or some knickknack blocking his line of sight." I grab my shower things. "I'm going to take a quick shower."

Mitchell nods. "I'll scramble some eggs."

"Thanks." I spend my entire shower thinking about how every lead in this case brings us to the same dead end. We have no idea who the killer is. We've uncovered Amelia's secret relationship, Rebecca and Jax's secret relationship, Amelia's body, and Hugo Spencer's involvement with the killer, but I still don't know who the killer actually is.

As soon as I'm dressed, I head to the kitchen where Mitchell is plating up eggs. "I need to read the frying pan that killed Wilson McDonald. We don't know how he was connected to all of this, but he must have seen his killer's face."

Mitchell shakes his head. "There were no prints on the frying pan other than McDonald's."

Damn it! So anything I read off it would show me the killer's perspective again.

Mitchell hands me my plate, his free hand resting on my shoulder. "We'll figure it out. You're doing great."

"Please don't patronize me. You know I can't stand that."

He clears his throat. "Take your plate into the living room. I'll bring the coffee."

Jeffrey is back in his cage. "Why didn't you show me his face, huh?" I ask him once I put my plate on the coffee table.

"Don't even think about reading him again," Mitchell says, walking into the room.

"Last time I checked, you weren't my boss, Mitchell."

"As if you could actually work for anyone." He scoffs. "You'd be fired in a heartbeat."

"Excuse you, but I work with the WPD all the time. Including on this case."

"Notice you said 'with,' not 'for.' And look at how you reacted to Chief Johansen before you won him over."

"Speaking of, how is Officer Andrews? Anyone heard from him since he was suspended?"

"No, the station has been peaceful according to Wallace." Mitchell sits down and sips his coffee.

"All hell is going to break loose when he comes back. You know that, right?"

"I'm well aware, but I'm also not worried. Andrews will have to keep his rage on the down low so the chief doesn't come down on him again."

"Back to our case. I have a plan, but I'll need your help."

"Don't you always?" he flashes me a smile before shoveling eggs into his mouth.

I roll my eyes. "As I was saying, I need you to distract the crowd so I can read Hugo Spencer's body."

Mitchell drops his fork, and it clatters against the plate. "You want to read a dead man in his casket at his funeral?"

"I don't see that I have any other choice. Hugo was helping this guy, against his will, but still. He had to know him, which means he knew what he looks like." He might be the only one who did.

"One of these days, I'm going to lose my badge because of you."

"Yeah, yeah. You keep saying that, but until it happens, we're doing things my way."

"Don't we always?" His true implication isn't lost on me.

"Are you in or not?" I ask.

"I've got your back, partner. I just need you to promise me you aren't going to create a scene while Mrs. Spencer, who hired you to solve Hugo's murder by the way, is there to see it."

"When do I ever cause a scene?" I say with a smirk before sipping my coffee.

Mrs. Spencer opted to have the entire service in the cemetery instead of starting at the funeral home. Mitchell and I meet up with Dad near my grandmother's grave before the service. He was there with Mom, who isn't attending the service, opting to sit on the bench by Grandma Maywood's grave and visit instead.

It's hard for me to be by the grave, not because my grandmother was a psychic and pushed everyone she loved away, but because I was almost murdered standing there. Another reason why I hate Sam Pierce. It's tough to think about. I meet Mitchell's gaze. He saved my life that day, and I think that's when I realized that as much as he makes me angry, I'm totally falling for him.

He wraps his arm around my shoulder. "Come on. Let's get this over with."

I wave to Mom as the three of us start toward the

crowd forming by the green tent. "Thank you," I whisper to Mitchell. "Every time I'm there, I see that gun pointed at my head."

"So do I," he says, and his arm tugs me closer.

We pull apart when we approach the service. Mrs. Spencer walks over to us immediately.

"We're making progress on the case," I assure her, hoping she doesn't still blame me for her husband's death.

"I can't bear to think the one responsible is out there somewhere. He's walking free while my Hugo is—" Sobs cut her off, and I offer her my left hand. I'm really trying to get better at the whole physical contact thing.

There are rows of white folding chairs set up, and Mitchell and I take seats in the back during the service. I'll have to wait to read the body until people go up to pay their respects individually. Dad is hanging back, observing the crowd. I think he's convinced the killer is going to show up. But I know he won't. He's avoiding me like the plague. He wouldn't have enlisted Hugo's help in the first place if he wasn't. I feel like he was there that day at the prison, and Hugo was supposed to notify him if I showed up so the killer could get out of there.

That also means the killer is either in contact with O'Neil, threatening him out of talking to me anymore, or he's in contact with another inmate in case he needs O'Neil silenced. When this is all over, I'm going to need some answers from Levi O'Neil.

When it's our turn to approach the casket, Mitchell is

right at my side. "Fair warning, in order to block you from everyone else's view, I plan to wrap my arm around you again. My suit jacket should hide your right arm and hand."

"You don't have to warn me about doing things like that, Mitchell. I can't read you when you aren't touching my right hand."

"Yeah, but I'm still touching you, and I know you're not a big fan of touching."

Did he not notice how many times he's touched me recently? Or how many times I've touched him? Maybe he doesn't because it's not as big a deal for him as it is for me. There are three people in line before us, so I turn to face him. "You know you had your arm around me on the way over here, right?"

"I'm aware." He leans down and whispers, "Why? Did you think you were daydreaming?"

"Oh, good Lord." I roll my eyes. "Just when I think you're capable of acting like a normal human being..."

He laughs, and several people jerk their heads in our direction. He immediately stops and holds up a hand in apology.

"Nice going," I whisper.

"What can I say? You tend to make me forget there's an entire world going on around us." He looks down at the ground as soon as the words come out of his mouth. I'm starting to think it's becoming really embarrassing for him that he has no inner filter. Maybe I have nothing to worry about as far as accidentally reading him and seeing something he doesn't want me to see, because he doesn't seem to be able to keep anything from me anymore.

We're next in line, and I step up to the casket, which is only open on the lower half. I've never seen a casket closed in reverse like this, but seeing as Hugo was shot in the head, it makes sense. Mitchell takes his place on my right side and wraps his arm around me. But this time, his arm isn't around my shoulders. It's around my waist. To everyone here, we look like a couple.

"Ready?" he asks me.

I swallow hard before placing my hand on Hugo's.

"O'Neil told me all about you."

"I doubt that," the killer laughs through the phone. "He'd never tell you about me. Other than I need your assistance. And I'm sure he told you the consequences if you choose not to cooperate."

"Leave my wife out of this. I'll do what you say. Where should we meet?"

"We won't be meeting. There's no need for you to know who I am. I just need to know if and when that psychic P.I. and her detective friend show up at the prison. O'Neil's been causing trouble. He enjoys these games, but he can't outsmart me. I'll win, just like I always do. That's how he wound up there after all."

"Piper," Mitchell's voice snaps me out of the vision. "People are starting to stare."

I remove my hand from Hugo, and Mitchell and I

walk off to the back of the crowd to join Dad. "Hugo never met the killer in person. He has no idea who he is. Apparently, O'Neil liked to play games to try to one-up the killer. That's what this is. And the killer is playing right along to show O'Neil he's better than he is. The consequence for losing the first time around was O'Neil confessing to a murder he didn't commit."

"O'Neil is probably laughing at the fact that we have people protecting him. He's not really in danger at all," Dad says. "He orchestrated this. Set it all in motion."

"What is it with killers and games?" Mitchell asks. He's about to say something else when his phone rings. He pulls it from inside his suit jacket. "Brennan." His eyes widen. "We'll be right there." He hangs up and shoves the phone back in his pocket. "Rebecca Crane found Jax Dawson murdered in his home this morning."

CHAPTER TWENTY-ONE

We get to Jax's house just as the CSI team is finishing up. Rebecca is sitting on the couch in the living room, crying. Since I don't like seeing dead bodies, I opt to talk to her first.

Mitchell and Dad head into the bedroom to check out where Jax was murdered.

"Rebecca, where's Jacob?" I ask, because as much as I want to believe Jacob isn't Amelia's killer, he still could be. And even if he's not, he could have finally reached the end of his tolerance for his wife's affair. He'd never hurt her, but I don't think he cares about Jax anymore at all.

"Jacob went to the office this morning. That's why I'm here. Jax and I were supposed to have a date."

"So you found him?"

She nods. "I have a key to the back door. That's the

way I always come in. He usually waits for me in bed, so I went into the bedroom, not knowing anything was wrong. He was just lying there, staring up at the ceiling. And his neck is red, like someone..."

He was strangled. Just like Amelia. I have to see the body. I have to read it so I can finally ID this killer, because it has to be the same person.

"Will you be okay on your own for a moment? I'd like to go get a read off the crime scene."

She nods.

I stand up and head into the bedroom, which is on the first floor at the back of the house. Mitchell sees me before I even step into the room. It's like he's developed Piper radar or something. I step around Dad and walk toward the bed.

"That's how he was when I got here," Rebecca says behind me. I didn't realize she'd followed me.

Jax was clearly awake when he was attacked because the position of his body indicates he was standing at the foot of the bed when he was strangled. He probably fell back onto the mattress after he died. Like Rebecca said, there are marks on Jax's neck.

Mitchell approaches me and whispers, "You have to admit this makes Jacob Crane look extremely guilty. Is there any way you misread him, Piper?"

"I thought the same thing at first but not anymore. I think Jax was killed because the killer figured out Jax and

Rebecca saw him that day at the theater. He's trying to get rid of witnesses, which means Rebecca is in danger until we catch him."

Mitchell nods. "Do your thing. I'll talk to Wallace about getting police protection for Rebecca until this is over."

"Thanks. Go easy on her. This is going to out the affair, and while I feel it should be outed, she's showing emotion, which is very much unlike her."

"Are you tapping into your empath side and channeling her emotions?"

"Quite possibly," I say before moving toward Jax. I'm thankful he's wearing pajama bottoms. His chest is bare, though. I opt to read his hand and take it in mine.

"Who the hell are you?" Jax says. "And how did you get in here?"

"You don't recognize me?" The man is wearing a baseball cap, a dark T-shirt, and dark jeans.

"No. Should I?"

"See the problem is I don't know if you're telling the truth or not."

"Look, I don't know what you're after, but you need to get the hell out of my house before I physically remove you."

He laughs. "I'm a lot stronger than I look. Let me show you." He reaches for Jax's neck and squeezes.

Jax fights back, kicking and swinging at the man. But

the killer says, "I think I hear Rebecca. She's just in time to join the party."

Jax falls for it and stops fighting back just long enough for the killer to knee him between the legs. Jax starts to crumble to the ground, only held up by the hands around his neck. Instead of fighting, he tries to yell Rebecca's name, but it's garbled as the killer squeezes even harder.

"Piper, you're okay."

I open my eyes at the sound of Mitchell's voice. We're on the floor at the foot of the bed. And once again, I'm cradled in Mitchell's lap.

"What happened to her?" Rebecca asks.

Mitchell gets to his feet with me in his arms and carries me out into the living room. He lies me down on the couch and crouches down beside me. "You've got to start giving me a signal when things get bad in those visions."

I rub my throat, unable to talk.

Mitchell brushes my hair from my face. "Just relax. Judging by your reaction, I'm guessing Jax was strangled in a way that was very similar to Amelia."

I nod, which hurts my neck.

"Try not to move. Blink twice for yes, okay?" Mitchell says.

I blink twice.

"Did you see the killer?"

I blink twice.

"Did you recognize him?"

I frown and don't blink.

"I'm guessing Jax didn't call him by name."

Nothing again from me.

"Did Jax know him?"

Nothing.

"Okay. Sit tight. I'll get you some water." Mitchell leaves the room, and Rebecca walks over to me.

"The police said I have to have an officer watching me at all times until you catch this guy. Everything is going to be out in the open. How can it not be? Jacob will demand to know why I found Jax and why I'm in danger. But it won't change anything. Jax is gone. Jacob and I will get past this." Rebecca bends down and grips my forearm. "Here's a little advice, though." Her head jerks in the direction Mitchell went. "You've got a man there who worships the ground you walk on, and I've seen the way you look at him. Don't wait too long to tell him how you feel, or someone else will snatch him up."

I swallow hard before saying, "You knew Jax before Jacob."

She nods. "Jax was the one who introduced us. I didn't tell him how I felt until it was too late. Jacob proposed, and Jax wasn't going to stand in his way." She stands up.

"Dr. Crane," Officer Wallace says, "I'm ready to bring you home now." He nods at me and gives me a sympathetic look as he walks her out of the house.

Mitchell comes back with a glass of water for me, and I sit up so he can sit down beside me.

"Thank you," I say.

"Hey, look who's talking." He bumps his shoulder into mine.

I take a sip of water, relishing the feel of the cool liquid soothing my throat. My mind starts flipping through every clue we've uncovered. This person isn't connected to the theater. He didn't know Rebecca or Jacob Crane. He didn't know Jax Dawson. I have to go back further. What am I missing?

"Maybe we should talk to O'Neil again," Mitchell says. "Make him talk or read him against his will."

O'Neil. This all began with him. Him and his riddle. The bird. I grab Mitchell's hand, and his gaze meets mine. "The bird cage. O'Neil wanted us to go to Hilltop House. We have to go back there. We missed something."

Mitchell stands up and pulls me to my feet. I place the water on the coffee table as Dad walks into the living room. His gaze falls on Mitchell's and my hands. I'm still holding Mitchell's hand. I can't think about that now, though.

"Mitchell and I are going back to Hilltop House. There's something there that I missed," I tell Dad.

"I'll follow you."

We race out.

"Any idea what we're looking for?" Mitchell asks on the way.

"I think the killer knew Amelia through Hilltop House."

"But it's run by Theresa Hill, and all the foster kids are girls," Mitchell says. "The killer is male."

"Then he works there in some capacity. As a janitor or landscaper." *No.* "Damn it!"

"Are your senses arguing with you again?" Mitchell asks.

"Yes. I'm wrong about that."

"Are we still going?"

"Yes. The clue is there. Remember, O'Neil wants to win this game. He wouldn't have steered us in the wrong direction." What am I not seeing? I squeeze my thighs in frustration.

Mitchell reaches over and places his hand on mine. "Easy. I won't figure this out without you, so stop taking your frustration out on my partner."

"What should I do then?"

"Punch me," he says, his tone completely serious.

"I'm not punching you." I cross my arms.

"You want to smack me instead?"

"No. Stop it. I'm not hurting you in any way."

He smiles and keeps driving.

Dad somehow beats us to Hilltop House. "Glad to see you're driving carefully with my daughter in the car these days," he says when we meet him at the door.

If he only knew how Mitchell drove to the hospital the other day. Instead of responding, Mitchell rings the bell.

Theresa Hill smiles at Mitchell as soon as she opens the door. "Detective, what a lovely surprise."

I'm a little surprised myself when Mitchell doesn't go into flirt mode. Instead, he places his hand on my lower back. "Ms. Hill, Piper and I were hoping to have a look around at a few more of Amelia's old things."

Her eyes narrow at me. "I see." Her gaze goes to Dad. "And you are?"

"Thomas Ashwell."

She smiles at him. "Such a strong name, Thomas."

"A strong name for a happily married man," Dad says, and I smile.

"Won't you all come in?" she says, her tone flat.

She leads us upstairs again. "You already have the bird cage, which we would like back at some point, Detective," she says. "Most of Amelia's other belongings were clothing items, which were distributed between the girls. She did have a television that we use in the den."

"Could we see it?" Mitchell asks.

"Sure, but all the girls are in there at the moment."

I don't want to have a vision in a room full of teenage girls. We walk past a door I didn't notice the last time we were here.

The voice on the other side of the door sounds so familiar, but it's muffled so I can't place it. And then it whistles. "Who is that?" I ask Theresa.

"My brother. Why?"

My head whips in Mitchell's direction. I can't say

aloud what I now know to be true. Theresa Hill's brother was O'Neil's accomplice.

"I wasn't aware you had a brother," Mitchell says.

"He's a silent partner. He's rarely ever here. Most of the girls don't even know him. He prefers it that way. He says he doesn't want the recognition for helping those who are less fortunate." Theresa waves her hand in the air as if she can't understand not wanting credit for doing something good.

"What's his name?" I ask, trying to conceal my suspicions.

"Terrance."

"Is he older or younger than you?" Mitchell asks.

"Two years younger. Why?"

"We'd love to meet him," I say.

"I'm afraid he's busy at the moment. Our former accountant was murdered, and poor Terrance has been going crazy trying to find us a new one."

I grip Mitchell's arm. Wilson McDonald was the accountant for Hilltop House. That's how the killer knew him. McDonald must have suspected Terrance, and that's why he was killed! I have to get inside that office.

"I'm sure he's very busy, but this will only take a moment," Mitchell says, sensing my need to see the man behind that door and confirm it's the same man who killed Jax Dawson.

Theresa doesn't seem inclined to help Mitchell now

that she knows he's not interested in her. "I suppose you can wait downstairs. I'll let him know you're here."

My senses tingle. If she warns him we're here, he'll run. I don't care how rude it is, I grip the doorknob and force my way into the office.

"Ms. Ashwell!" Theresa yells, and at the sound of my name, Terrance jumps up and jerks the top drawer of his desk open.

"Freeze!" Mitchell yells, gun already drawn. "Put your hands in the air where I can see them."

Terrance glares at his sister. "You're useless. How could you let them in here?"

"What are you talking about? Terrance, what is going on?" she asks.

"Your brother was in a secret relationship with Amelia Crane," I say. "He discovered she had a large sum of money left to her by her parents, and he had big plans to get his hands on that money. He hired Levi O'Neil to stalk her and scare her enough so he could talk her into running away with him and giving him control of her money in the process." I turn to speak directly to Terrance. "But she didn't want to go through with your plan, so you killed her in a heated moment."

Mitchell walks around the desk. "Arms behind your back."

Terrance does as he's told.

"You knew your accountant, Wilson McDonald, was having some landscaping done. It was the perfect way to dispose of Amelia's body. You snuck over there and buried her while Wilson was out of the house. But when he questioned how that one area was so much more fertile than the rest, you were afraid he'd dig it up to find out why. So you killed him."

"Except you found Amelia anyway, Ms. Ashwell. You've been a huge thorn in my side thanks to O'Neil."

"He's been in prison for a crime you committed," I say.

"He wasn't innocent. He helped me with my plan. You didn't find out why Amelia was so scared that night, did you? You don't know what it was that made her finally crack."

I shake my head. "Fill in the blank for me."

"O'Neil attacked her. I saved her from him. He was going to kill her. He tried to. In an alley behind the theater. He had a gun. But I stopped him."

"Only to kill her yourself as soon as you brought her home," I say.

He scoffs. "The bitch deserved it. She could have run away with me. I didn't mind being with her. If I had her money, I wouldn't have had a reason to kill her."

"That just makes you a saint, doesn't it?" Mitchell says. He has Terrance cuffed.

"How did you find out Jax and Rebecca saw you in the movie theater all those years ago?" I ask.

"Easy. I've been following you. You were smart to bunk with the cop." Terrance jerks his head at Mitchell. "I think I even sparked a love connection between you two, so you're welcome for that."

"Shut up," Dad says. "You've been stalking my daughter, you murdered Amelia Crane, Hugo Spencer, Wilson McDonald, and Jax Dawson. You're going to prison for the rest of your sorry existence."

"You can say that again," Mitchell says before reading Terrance his rights.

CHAPTER TWENTY-TWO

I'm not sure who's happier to be back home, Jezebel or me. We're cuddled up on the couch, her head in my lap and a book in my hand, when there's a knock on the door.

"Come in," I say, knowing it's Mitchell.

He opens the door, and the smell of the Chinese food greets my senses. "I brought lunch."

"You're the best," I say, putting my bookmark in the book and placing it on the side table.

Jez jumps down from the couch to give Mitchell a proper hello.

"How's my favorite girl?" Mitchell asks her. He puts the food on the counter and bends down to scratch both sides of her face. He gets a big kiss in response.

"Give me the details," I say, walking into the kitchen to help Mitchell plate the food.

"Terrance was processed for all four murders. He pled guilty, which I suppose was his consequence for losing this game to O'Neil. O'Neil, on the other hand, has pleaded guilty to attempted murder now. He's not getting out of jail anytime soon. We're splitting up the duo. Terrance will be sent to a maximum-security prison in New Jersey."

"I guess the guards and the warden don't want to deal with those two scheming behind bars," I say.

"Exactly. How did Mrs. Spencer take the news?" he asks, pouring iced tea for us both.

"How you'd think. She's happy we caught Terrance and still grieving her dead husband. I didn't tell her Hugo was helping Terrance because Terrance threatened her. I want her to be able to move on from all this, and I figured that would give her nightmares for life."

"That was sweet of you, Piper."

"What can I say? Sometimes I can be thoughtful." I carry the two plates of food to the couch.

"I'm still not sure how Terrance was able to fool Amelia into dating him."

"I've been thinking about that," I say as I sit. I put the plates on the coffee table. "Amelia never suspected Terrance Hill of being the awful person he is because she thought the fact that he was helping out kids with nowhere else to go meant he had to have a good heart. Plus, he was her best friend's uncle. Of course, that was why she felt the need to hide the relationship. I'm pretty sure Terrance convinced her Olivia would never speak to either one of them again if she found out."

Mitchell sits beside me in Jez's usual spot. "So that meant they couldn't tell anyone, which was exactly what Terrance wanted."

"Yup. The guy had the whole thing planned out. He would have gotten away with it if O'Neil hadn't decided to get back at him."

Mitchell raises his glass of iced tea and hands me mine. "To another closed case."

I don't clink my glass with his. "We lost three people on this case. I don't really feel like celebrating."

"We saved Rebecca Crane and locked up a serial killer. I'm willing to celebrate that." He clinks his glass against mine. "Besides, there's something else to celebrate."

"What's that?" I cock my head at him.

"I'm pretty sure you admitted you like me."

"When did I do that?"

He puts down his glass and then takes mine and places it on the table as well. "Let's see. How about all the times when you didn't pull away from me or when you actually touched me. You held my hand more than once."

I open my mouth to make a witty comment about the case screwing with my head, but then I close it. I look down at Mitchell's hand on his leg, which is very close to mine. My pulse races as I reach for his hand and lace my fingers through it.

He stares at our hands and then meets my gaze. Part of me expects him to totally push his luck and try to kiss me. Instead, he says, "I was thinking we should take Jez to the new dog park."

Jez comes over with her tail wagging and places her head in Mitchell's lap.

"How does she understand everything?" he asks me.

"She's smart. Plus, she loves you."

"She does, doesn't she?" He smiles and pats her head, but he doesn't let go of my hand.

"I'm pretty sure all females love you, so don't act so surprised."

"Not all," he says, "but at least the important ones seem to like me. That's more than enough for me."

"We should eat before our food gets cold," I say, pulling my hand from his. I bring my plate onto my lap, but not before I see the look of disappointment on Mitchell's face. I let him in for about sixty seconds and then erected my wall again. I put the plate back on the table and turn to face him, our knees touching. "I'm sorry. I know I said I didn't want to talk about it, but I think it's almost worse not to. So, here it goes." I take a deep breath, but the words won't come to me. I'm about to berate myself for being such a coward when I get a better idea. Very slowly, I lean forward and press my lips to Mitchell's. It's the softest, barely-there kiss in the history of kisses, I'm sure—even though I'm not the expert on kissing by any means. When I pull away, I smile, because I didn't accidentally read him or throw myself at him. Maybe Mitchell was right about us all along.

"I like your method of talking," he says with a smirk.

I laugh, and I can feel my cheeks heating up.

Mitchell runs his thumb over my right cheek. "Don't be embarrassed."

It takes all my effort to hold his gaze. "I've never..." I can't bring myself to tell him I've never made the first move before.

"Do you want to punch me now? You can if it will make you feel better."

Jez whines, and I pet her, cupping her face in my hand.

"Jezebel is right. There will be no punching."

"More kissing?" Mitchell asks with a boyish charm that almost makes me give in. Almost.

"Tell me more about the dog park."

He dips his head and then looks into my eyes. "Are you pushing me away again?"

"Since I'm planning on going with you, I'd say no, I'm not."

He laces his fingers through mine. "Piper Ashwell, are you saying this will be an official date? One where other people would see us together and we wouldn't be pretending?"

I say something I've never said before in my life. "Yes, it's a date." Lord help us both!

If you enjoyed the book, please consider leaving a review. And look for *Great Crimes Read Alike*, coming soon!

You can stay up-to-date on all of Kelly's releases by subscribing to her newsletter: http://bit.ly/2pvYT07

ALSO BY USA TODAY BESTSELLING AUTHOR KELLY HASHWAY

Piper Ashwell Psychic P.I. Series

A Sight For Psychic Eyes

A Vision A Day Keeps the Killer Away

Read Between the Crimes

Drastic Crimes Call for Drastic Insights

You Can't Judge a Crime by its Aura

Fortune Favors the Felon

Murder is a Premonition Best Served Cold

It's Beginning to Look a Lot Like Murder

Good Visions Make Good Cases (Novella collection)

A Jailbird in the Vision Is Worth Two In The Prison

Great Crimes Read Alike

I Spy With My Psychic Eye Someone Dead

A Vision in Time Saves Nine

Never Smite the Psychic That Reads You

There's No Crime Like the Prescient

Fight Fire With Foresight

Madison Kramer Mystery Series

Manuscripts and Murder

Sequels and Serial Killers

Fiction and Felonies

Cup of Jo

Coffee and Crime

Macchiatos and Murder

Cappuccinos and Corpses

Frappes and Fatalities

Lattes and Lynching

Glaces and Graves

Espresso and Evidence

Paranormal Books:

Touch of Death (Touch of Death #1)

Stalked by Death (Touch of Death #2)

Face of Death (Touch of Death #3)

The Monster Within (The Monster Within #1)

The Darkness Within (The Monster Within #2)

Unseen Evil (Unseen Evil #1)

Evil Unleashed (Unseen Evil #2)

Into the Fire (Into the Fire #1)

Out of the Ashes (Into the Fire #2)

Up in Flames (Into the Fire #3)

Dark Destiny

Fading Into the Shadows

The Day I Died

Replica

ACKNOWLEDGMENTS

I'm fortunate to have the best support team on this series. Patricia Bradley, your insights on these stories would give Piper a run for her money. Thank you for believing in me and these characters. Ali Winters at Red Umbrella Graphic Designs, you continue to amaze me with gorgeous cover after gorgeous cover. To my family, thank you for putting up with me when I hibernate to finish a book. To my VIP reader group, Kelly's Cozy Corner, you guys are amazingly supportive. And finally, thank you to everyone who reads this book and the others in this series. You allow me to keep thinking up more adventures for Piper and Mitchell.

ABOUT THE AUTHOR

Kelly Hashway fully admits to being one of the most accident-prone people on the planet, but luckily she gets to write about female sleuths who are much more coordinated than she is. Maybe it was growing up watching *Murder, She Wrote* that instilled a love of mystery, but she spends her days writing cozy mysteries. Kelly's also a sucker for first love, which is why she writes romance under the pen name Ashelyn Drake. When she's not writing, Kelly works as an editor and also as Mom, which she believes is a job title that deserves to be capitalized.

facebook.com/KellyHashwayCozyMysteryAuthor

twitter.com/kellyhashway

instagram.com/khashway

bookbub.com/authors/kelly-hashway

www.ingramcontent.com/pod-product-compliance
Lightning Source LLC
Chambersburg PA
CBHW020335310726
48979CB00015B/2375/J

* 9 7 8 1 9 5 3 8 0 0 1 5 2 *